PROLOGUE

FOUR DECADES AGO...

"PAY ATTENTION!"

The sharp rap of the ruler across knuckles brought tears to Luna's eyes, but she knew better than to cry. The nuns who ran the orphanage didn't tolerate whining or misbehavior.

Her crime? She'd been caught staring out the window, longing for the sunshine and fresh air just out of reach. How she missed it. Day in and day out, the orphans went from the dormitory to the classroom or the church then back to the dorm. That schedule allowed for only a short outdoor break where they could breathe fresh air and stretch their legs. Not enough for a growing girl—and torture for the wolf inside.

Before Luna could earn another bruise from the strict nun, she ducked her head and resumed practicing her cursive letters then moved on to mathematics and science, followed by an hour of prayer before dinner, chores, and more prayer as they readied for bed.

Every day was the same. Despite being here just a few weeks, Luna barely remembered a time before the orphanage and its strict schedule. Only her mother's face, and her yipped admonishment to run the last time Luna had seen her, remained clear.

Luna had run, even as she'd heard the gunshots. She'd run and run, until she could run no more. When a pair of hikers found her, she'd been naked and covered in scratches. The strangers had brought her to town and dropped her off at the police station, where a uniformed man with a big, bushy mustache questioned her, his burly manner frightening to a small child.

The kinder social worker had better luck getting answers.

"Who are you?"

"Luna Smith."

"Where are your parents?"

ROGUE
UNLOVED

Feral Pack: Book Four

EVE LANGLAIS

"I lost my mom in the woods."

"Where do you live?"

"I don't know."

They'd moved so often and rarely stayed in one place for long. They'd even lived in a car, until the engine died. They'd been walking ever since. It had been a while since Luna had been in school.

A different social worker had temporarily placed Luna in a foster home while they'd searched for her mother. For three days, the police searched, only to fail to find her mama. Given Luna's age—seven, with a birthday coming up in the fall—they'd chosen to transfer her from the foster home, which was better suited for younger children, to an orphanage run by nuns.

She hated it.

Every day, Luna hoped her mother would appear and take her away from this cold and scary place. However, no one came to rescue Luna.

At least not all the sisters were mean. Some could be quite nice and comforting to a little girl, but they didn't smell right. Nor did they hug Luna when she was sad. Or care when she wanted more meat to eat instead of oatmeal and stew.

When the full moon rolled around, the first since her arrival—the last being the night she'd lost Mama

—Luna thought nothing of sitting in the dormitory window to admire it. It tickled her skin. She closed her eyes, basking in it. Her wolf wanted to come out and play, but Luna knew better. Mama always said to keep it a secret.

"What are you doing out of bed?" The harsh rebuke came from Sister Francine, one of the younger but more severe nuns.

"I was admiring the moon. It's so pretty." Luna pointed at it.

"The moon is for those who love the devil. Do you worship Satan?"

Luna gaped. She hadn't even known about God and the devil before she'd arrived at the orphanage. That ignorance had led to an old man in robes flinging water in her face and chanting. A baptism the nuns called it, to ensure her soul didn't go to Hell if she died.

"No, Sister Francine, I would never worship the devil."

"And yet, here you are, doing his work, out of bed, obviously praying to him."

The accusation confused her. "But I—"

"Don't you sass me!"

Luna couldn't avoid the switch the sister wielded —freshly cut every day so as to keep them in line. It whipped against her bare arms peeking from the nightdress.

"Ow." She couldn't stop the sharp exclamation.

"That didn't hurt."

"It did," Luna insisted, lips wobbling as tears brimmed. Mama had never hit her. No one had. This kind of pain was new.

"Liar! Devil's handmaiden." The switch came down again and again, even as the moon seemed to get brighter.

Luna's pain and fear swirled into anger. This was unfair. Why was she being punished for something she used to do every full moon with Mama?

"I hate you," Luna screamed.

As Sister Francine brought down the lash again, Luna grabbed for the switch, her little hands gripping it tight.

The act of defiance led to a rapid slap that snapped her head back, and her teeth clacked hard, nipping her tongue. She tasted blood, and more tears welled.

She might be young, but she knew what Francine was doing was wrong. Evil. And according to the nuns, the Bible said to fight evil. She knew only one way to do that.

As her anger exploded, so did her wolf.

Caught in a rage, wanting only to stop the pain—not just that of her whipped hands and arms but the pain in her sad heart too—Luna found satisfaction for her frustration. It took strident screaming from the other orphans for her to snap out of it. By the time the other nuns arrived, Sister Francine was crawling to the door, bleeding from the many scratches and bite marks peppered all over her body.

The shock in the gazes of those around Luna fizzled her anger and shriveled her up inside, because she saw fear and disgust. They thought her a monster.

And perhaps she was. No one else had blood in their mouth.

She deflated, fur receding, skin reappearing, a weak child once more.

The nuns lunged, and Luna didn't fight them as they dragged her from the dormitory to a storage room, where they locked her in. She hugged her bare knees—she'd lost her nightgown when she'd shifted. Not for the first time, she had no blanket to cover her. But before, she'd had Mama. Now, she was alone.

The days after were a blur that involved forced prayer overseen by various nuns that left her knees raw and her voice hoarse. She went to the bathroom in a bucket, though not often, as they fed her only once a day and only barely.

According to the nuns, something was wrong with Luna. *She worships the devil*, some whispered. *Monster,* said others. They made the cross every time they saw her and never made eye contact. They feared and hated her.

The priest who'd flung water at her returned, this time to cast out the demon he claimed possessed her. He doused her in holy water. Fasted with her. Prayed for an annoying amount of time. Did God really listen to such inane prattle? Daily, he demanded Luna renounce the devil. In hopes of stopping the torture, she agreed. She'd do anything to get out of the closet. They told her she would be released only after she proved herself at the next full moon.

She might have succeeded in holding in her wolf, except the nuns thought it a brilliant idea to force her to confront the devil's embrace—which, in her case, was moonlight.

They forced her to kneel on the stone slabs inside the chapel. The thin material of her pants barely cushioned her knees against the hard surface. Hands clasped, she prayed as the sun went down, illuminating the stained glass and framing the cross with the hanging figure of Jesus.

She prayed right through dinner, her throat parched. Her knees hurt. She couldn't stop. If she could prove she'd cast out the devil, if she kept her wolf inside, she would gain her freedom.

She just had to be strong.

Hail Mary…

The moon rose, glinting through the windows on the east side, bathing her in its silvery light.

Luna held firm against the urge within.

…full of grace.

She repeated the words to the rosary over and over, a fast whisper that was working. She was in control. She could hide like Mama had told her to.

"Repent!" The shout came with a slap that rocked her head hard.

Luna bit her tongue, and coppery blood flavored her mouth.

She started over with her prayer. "Hail Mary—"

"Repent the devil," Sister Francine screamed before grabbing Luna's hair and tugging uncomfortably.

It hurt, and by the mad glint in the sister's eyes, Luna knew that the pain would get worse. And no one would stop her. Those watching did not interfere.

"Repent, unclean minion of Lucifer."

"No."

"What did you say, Satan's handmaiden?" Francine hissed.

"I said, no more."

"You don't get to say when I'm done." Francine gripped Luna's hair tighter.

The pain served only to make Luna's wolf stronger.

"You might want to run," was Luna's soft advice.

She called her wolf. Welcomed it amidst the screams of "Monster!"

That night, she was. Luna rampaged first through the church then the orphanage, snapping at anyone who confronted her. She wanted to escape, and yet, despite their fear, the nuns wouldn't unlock the doors. The windows were barred.

Eventually, Luna became too exhausted to fight.

She passed out, waking when the nuns, some of them obviously wounded, dragged her naked and exhausted body back to the closet.

Three days later, during which no one came even to feed her, the professor arrived, a kindly older gentleman who smiled at Luna and said, "Come with me, child."

She eyed him with suspicion.

"I'm Dr. Adams. I'm here because I heard about your unusual circumstances. I think I can help you."

"Can you find my mama?" In her mind, that was the only thing that could end this nightmare.

"I can try. In the meantime, you can stay with me. I have a room that's perfect for a young lady like yourself."

His kind expression and offer tempted her.

The nun at the door muttered, "Don't know why he wants the monster."

Tears pricked her eyes. *I'm not a monster.*

Dr. Adams knelt to eye level with her, and as if he read her mind, he said, "You're just misunderstood. Come with me. I promise you won't ever have to deal again with the sisters."

A promise she couldn't refuse.

When he reached out a hand, she dumbly took it.

What followed weren't years she cared to remember, and to this day, they'd left their mark.

She managed to keep the damage a secret until the day a depraved human hunter forced her to shift into the monster that had been hiding inside her for decades.

ONE

THE PRESENT.

WOW, *did I majorly fuck up.*

Luna had gravely miscalculated. Not something that happened often, and yet, as she faced a human hunter thought long dead, she faced a harsh truth. She'd been betrayed. Not just her, though, but all of Werekind.

The man in front of her, one Gerard Kline, hadn't just captured her. For decades now, he'd been sadistically killing her kind. And he'd gotten away with it because he'd had help. By Gerard's own admission, someone highly placed in the Lykosium Council, which regulated all things Were and the lesser-known others, had been giving Gerard help. Someone Luna and everyone else trusted had facilitated genocide, and they would pay dearly for it. Right after she killed Gerard and silenced his flapping lips.

At times like these, she really wished she weighed a few more pounds.

Eyeing the male in front of her, Luna gauged his strength versus hers. She had no weapon, and a quick check showed that the overconfident Gerard lacked a gun. All he had was a glass of booze on the tall pub table and two pouches. She'd have to act fast, before his paid soldiers interfered.

As she bolted toward him, her backup, a grizzly and grumpy Were named Lochlan, leaped for the kill. Gerard moved faster than expected, his hand slipping into an open pouch and emerging to fling some powder.

The beautiful wolf hit the floor, unconscious. Not dead. Not yet.

Gerard smirked at Luna in triumph. "They never learn. Want a turn?" He dug his hand into the other pouch.

"As a matter of fact, I do," she muttered.

Determined to not suffer the same fate, Luna held her breath as she passed through the handful of dust flung by Gerard. It glittered as it momentarily hung in the air like a cloud. Not one iota entered her mouth or nose. However, it settled on her bare hands and face.

Before she'd even blinked, her skin absorbed the powder and the ripping pain as fire coursed through her veins tore a scream from her throat. The chemical chain reaction happening in her body burned, and she gasped as it forced her to shift, something she'd not done in a long, long time—and for good reason.

Luna tried to hold it back. To not let herself lose control.

Her jaw cracked as it reshaped, and as the beast within shoved her out of the driver's seat, she uttered a long, eerie howl.

Now we're fucked.

That was her last coherent thought before she became a monster.

TWO

THE BEAST EMERGED FROM HER LONG SLUMBER and roared. It felt good to be free at last. Free to run, fight. Hunt...

Hunger tightened her belly. She eyed the two-legged, soft-skinned prey in front of her. He returned her stare, eyes wide with fear, and retreated like a coward. Smelled like food to her.

She lunged, and her claws sliced through flesh. Blood flowed, and the coppery tang woke her taste-buds. How long since she'd eaten fresh meat?

Too long.

Not long enough. Her thought and yet not at the same time.

The male screamed and tried to stem the flow of blood from his wound. Noisy creature. She batted again, knocking him to the floor, and might have had a nibble if not for an intruding scent. A reminder that she had another task.

My pup is in danger.

Kit.

The name had no meaning, but it came with a need to protect.

With a roar, she barreled toward the window. Glass shattered as she slammed through, the slices to her furred skin mere stinging inconveniences.

Once outside, she lifted her head and howled, a warning to those hunting her pup, a clarion call as well that she was coming to the rescue.

Following her pup's scent, she dashed for the woods wreathed in shadows and moist with dew. She didn't run alone. A wolf followed, his scent familiar. Very pleasing.

Mine.

Her mate, who remained as yet unmarked. She would rectify that, but only once she'd secured her pup.

Kit.

Once more, the name floated in her mind, along with the image of his red fur. The cognition fled just as quickly. She had no need for words when she had scent and sight.

As she weaved through the forest, the many diverging smells kept her on track. She counted many of the soft-fleshed, two-legged prey. Almost masked by their scent was that of her pup.

A choice to make. Track down her pup or hunt the soft-fleshed that would cause harm?

Eliminate the threat, and her pup would be safe. *Kill. Kill.*

The craving for blood and violence gave her speed. She tore through the woods, sometimes loping on all four legs, other times upright and leaping over obstacles in her path.

Movement drew her gaze and a toothy smile. Her prey thought he could hide. He didn't realize she could smell the stink of his fear. Hear the panicked huff of his breath.

She stalked the male whose trembling hands held a long-barreled object she knew to be a gun.

Duck, you idiot.

The weapon boomed, and she snarled as pain bloomed in her shoulder. But it was short-lived, like the culprit. A single swipe of her claws ended his life.

The next male she hunted tried to run. He didn't escape. She slammed into the two-legged threat and soon had a mouth full of blood. One by one, she killed all those who thought they could hurt her pup. She was a huntress, and none could escape her.

When no foes remained, she raised her muzzle to the moon and bayed her victory.

I've won. The enemy was dead, and a pressure within pulsed.

Yes, you've won. Now it's time to go back to sleep.

She shook her head. No. She'd already napped for too long. She wanted to be free.

The other voice insisted, *Enough. Give me back my body.*

She ran from the demand, as if racing would help. The silver wolf kept pace. Not too close, but near enough to keep her in sight. Her mate had wisely hung back as she'd hunted, keeping watch over her. Admiring her prowess.

She emerged from the woods to find a pond, the water still and reflecting. She stood over it. On two legs, not four like the wolf at her back or her pup.

As she dipped down to drink, she saw herself in the water, long jutting teeth, glowing eyes. *I'm a monster.* The pressure within screamed loud enough that she howled.

A deep voice behind her drawled, "Enough of that."

She whirled and bared her teeth at the wolf who was now a man.

Her mate didn't seem impressed and arched a brow. "Gonna eat my face too?"

Given his delectable scent, she wanted to eat him all right. Her gaze dropped.

His hands cupped his groin. "I am not that kind of sausage."

She huffed hotly in amusement and a bit of disagreement. He definitely had some meat she'd enjoy.

"I see you can understand me."

She did, and yet, she was so confused. Something wasn't right.

I'm not a monster.

She howled once more.

"Yeah, I can see you're frustrated. But the good news is that what happened to you is temporary. We'll have to wait until the effects of the drug wear off."

More words that she grasped yet didn't. The pressure within pulsed, and she slapped at her temples with her paws, as if that would make the voice inside disappear.

It didn't.

Give me back my body.

The hand her mate placed on her shoulder almost got bitten off. Her lip curled as he withdrew it.

"Calm down, sweetheart."

The comment had her growling and leaning closely enough that she could have eaten his face.

The big, two-legged man didn't budge.

"You wanna fight?"

She wanted something. The turmoil inside her needed an outlet.

He understood. "I can see you've got too much energy still. Guess we'd better let you work it out. Wanna wrestle?" He rolled his shoulders and cracked his human knuckles.

She yipped in amusement. As if he could think to—

He moved quickly and trickily. She found herself gripped and flung. As she sailed through the air, she flipped and landed with her hind legs bent. Her gaze narrowed on the man. Not with anger, but with interest. Perhaps she shouldn't underestimate him. After all, it stood to reason her mate would be the strongest and fastest of men.

"You gonna give me pretty eyes all day, or are we gonna play?" he cajoled with beckoning fingers.

Despite realizing it was most likely a trick, she

rushed him. He didn't move aside, but grunted as she drove her shoulder into his gut. He grabbed her, and she snapped as he once more tossed her to the ground.

This time, she rose more slowly and eyed him, looking for a weakness. His solid build might have no fur, and he had no claws, but the slabs of muscle showed his strength.

Rather than rashly pounce, she extended her paws with their furry claw-tipped fingers. He met her challenge, his own digits wrapping around her forearms as they pushed and heaved, a contest of determination that had them both huffing.

He surprised her by drawing her close to his body and twisting her so he pressed against her backside. Flesh against her fur. It excited, and she uttered a low rumble as her interest scented the air.

"Like fuck. Not while you're in this shape," he gasped and flung her away from him.

As she paced, his expression turned wary. She rushed in, and they wrestled again. She could have hurt him a few times, but she chose to not claw him. This was her mate after all, and he shouldn't be hurt. At the same time, she wasn't about to just give in.

He hooked his leg around hers, and they fell to the ground, locked together, rolling, heaving and grunting. While she might be more powerful, he proved slippery and tricky. At one point, he managed to flip her and land atop. He pinned her, his heavy weight holding her in place. She could have bucked free. Instead, she went still.

They stared at each other.

"Feeling calmer now, sweetheart?"

Not calm. She leaned forward and nuzzled his neck.

He tensed. "Be gentle," he reminded firmly.

Not liking the admonishment and intoxicated by his scent, she bit him.

THREE

"WHAT THE EVER-LOVING FUCK?" LOCHLAN yelled as Luna bit him.

By the time he'd flung himself away, she'd already managed to get in a good chomp of his flesh. He slapped a hand against the broken skin and growled. "Not cool, sweetheart."

An unapologetic Luna, still in her two-legged hybrid shape, bounded to her feet and snarled, impressive given all her teeth, including two over-sized, saber-like canines.

Once more, her gaze dropped to his cock, and he hated the fact he was semi aroused. Blame her scent. He didn't need to be shifted to smell her interest. But not only was he not into furry fucking, he also knew sex with Luna would be a mistake.

"Ain't happening, sweetheart," he drawled. "We both know we'd regret it."

Despite her wildness, caused by the drug that had forced her to shift only halfway, she understood enough to not like his reply. With a sharp bark, she bolted into the woods.

Again? He sighed. He didn't want to chase her, but what choice did he have?

"Fuck me," he muttered.

Lochlan was having a hell of a day. Fuck, a hell of a week. He should have never left the ranch where he'd gotten comfortable. Should have never gone on a road trip that had led him to the woods filled with camouflaged hunters, all dead because a crazed Luna, a woman he'd met only days ago, had gone on a rampage.

As to why he'd ended up there in the first place?

Poppy, a girl he thought of as the daughter he'd never had and a member of his Pack, had needed his help, and he couldn't say no. It was supposed to be a simple mission. Find a hunter named Gerard living in the woods and end his depraved ass. Instead, they'd all been captured.

It turned out they'd underestimated Gerard. The guy hadn't just hired a few warm bodies as security, he'd engaged the services of a militia group to protect him at his hunting lodge. Gerard had had good reason to need security, given he'd been abducting Were so he and his friends could hunt them. The man, utter scum, needed to be handled.

The attack by Lochlan and a gang that included Hammer, Luna, Darian, and Poppy had turned into an ambush. Lochlan had woken chained to the wall of a basement full of cages with people inside. His people. Shapeshifters like him, who hadn't deserved to be treated like animals.

Chained alongside him had been Luna. He'd first met her only days ago. Days he'd spent fighting an instant attraction. Days in which he'd come to the reluctant realization she was his mate.

Ugh. Definitely not something he'd had an interest in, despite the way he'd kept sliding glances at Luna when they'd both been tied up.

She was a fine-looking woman, around his age with interesting eyes and attitude. He'd thought that the sooner he freed her and the others, the quicker he could escape her disturbing presence—before he found himself sniffing her butt, or worse.

As if he that weren't enough to deal with, that prick Gerard had tossed a powder at Luna that forced her to shift.

And by *shift*, he didn't mean into a wolf. Okay,

not entirely accurate. She *was* a wolf, in the way a dinosaur was related to a crocodile. That was, she had the fur, the elongated muzzle, the ears, and the snarling, but then add in the fact she could stand upright, had saber-like teeth and claws like a honey badger, and well...

She'd become even more interesting.

Dangerous.

Kind of murder-y.

And, because of the whole mate thing, his responsibility.

Lochlan had shadowed and watched as Luna— aka Mega Werewolf—had ribboned the hunter who'd captured them. When she'd bolted from the house, she hadn't been hard to follow. For one thing, there had been plenty of screams and, yes, blood. But even without that, he would have tracked her easily because of her scent. He'd followed her as she'd single-handedly—or would that be single-pawedly?— taken out a group of armed men.

Then she'd led him on a merry chase that had ended up with them wrestling and her chomping on his flesh. Not an I-want-to-rip-out-your-throat kind of bite but the marking kind that some old-school werewolves liked to indulge in to show their claim on their mate.

And she'd done it to him.

Which meant the mate thing wasn't one-sided, as he'd hoped. How could this be happening?

And where the hell had she fucked off to now?

With yet another long-suffering sigh of annoyance, Lochlan tracked Luna. She hadn't gone far. He found her curled under a tree, lying on some soft moss, lightly snoring in exhaustion. She'd most likely wake up starving. Killing people always gave him an appetite.

He crouched by her side and said her name softly. "Luna? Come on, sweetheart. We have to get back to the others."

Luna kept napping.

"Seriously. Wake the fuck up. I am getting too old to be lugging limp bodies around." Usually his drunk friends. It took a lot to get a Were drunk, given their metabolism, but with dedication and moonshine, it could be done.

At least she didn't weigh as much as Hammer or Amarok. He'd have to carry her only until he found Kit. Let the kid take care of his mom. Not his job.

Lochlan simply wanted to go back home, where a woman with the oddest eyes and sweetest scent wouldn't be there to remind him of what he could never have.

Her only reaction when he scooped her into his arms? A soft grumble and a nuzzle of his skin. Luna proved lighter than he'd expected, despite her expanded, furry shape.

As he toted her in his arms, he noticed a hush in the forest. Not completely out of place, given the battle that had just happened. Still, he shifted his grip on Luna so she hung over his shoulder, making it easier for him to jog.

Danger prickled at his nape. His senses switched to high alert even as he heard and saw nothing untoward.

The intrusion came from above. A figure, dressed in black from head to foot, dropped to the ground and aimed a gun at his chest. From behind a concealing balaclava, the person barked, "Drop her."

Lochlan cocked his head. "I don't think so." He sniffed to try to get a sense of the man-shaped stranger with a deep voice. There was no scent. One of Gerard's people? Or someone else? "Who are you?"

"None of your business."

"It kind of is my business, because if you're with that fucktard Gerard, well, then we have a problem."

"I work for the Lykosium and have orders to retrieve the female you're carrying."

"You're here on orders from the Lykosium?" Lochlan repeated the information only because it had caught him by surprise. "Prove it." He'd learned his lesson long ago to never blindly obey, especially when something about a situation felt off.

The masked stranger snapped, "I don't have to prove anything. Hand her over now, or face the consequences."

"Why do you want her? Has she committed a crime?"

"The reason doesn't concern you."

The stranger was right. It didn't. Still... Something reeked worse than the swamp past the easternmost pasture. "Do you know who she is?" he asked. Neither of them had called her by name.

"Luna Smith, Lykosium Council member, and my orders are to retrieve her by any means necessary." The clear threat was accompanied by the shifting of the gun so that it aimed at Lochlan's head.

It would be easy to hand her over and wash his hands of the situation.

She's defenseless. And he wouldn't feel right handing her over while she was unconscious. Especially to a stranger. "How do I know you're not one of the hunter's buddies?"

"I'm not part of the group she killed. She will answer for her actions here today."

"Answer for what? She saved Were lives."

"She wasn't supposed to be here."

That arched his brows. "Meaning what exactly? Because if she'd not shown up, then a whole lot of our kind would be dead right now."

"Enough of this. You've been given ample warning. Either comply or face the consequences." The muzzle of the gun gave a clue as to what those would be.

Lochlan had garnered enough from this conversation to know: a) he didn't like this fucker; b) he wasn't handing Luna over; and c) either Lochlan or this masked stranger wouldn't be leaving this forest alive. Hopefully, this fucker's will was up to date.

"Fuck you, asshole." Lochlan didn't even pretend to play nice.

"Wrong answer." As the man started to put pressure on the trigger, Lochlan silently apologized to Luna and tossed her at the guy.

The stranger startled and jerked as he fired off a wild shot, giving Lochlan enough time to tackle his ass to the ground. He quickly gained the upper hand, only to curse as he realized the guy wasn't alone.

The first bullet seared past his shoulder, and he

hissed. He rolled before the second was fired. It took him only a moment to spot the sniper up a tree, taking aim. He ran in a zigzag, hating that his dick and balls were flopping. However, this proved to be a case where four legs wouldn't work as well as two. Because wolves couldn't climb.

He leaped for the branch below the shooter, who aimed down and missed again. Lochlan let go of the limb he'd bent, and it slapped the one above it. The sniper lost their footing and fell, hitting their head hard against a rock. That worked.

As Lochlan whirled, he saw the first assailant taking aim. He fired, his weapon set on automatic. *Rat-tat-tat*. Lochlan grunted as a slug hit him in the shoulder. Fuck. He dropped to the ground, scrabbling for cover, which was when two more fuckers joined the party.

"Where did he go?"

"In the bushes."

Which led to more blind firing—at the wrong bush, though it wouldn't take long before they realized that. Not to mention he'd left Luna behind.

His shoulder throbbed, but he ignored it as he mentally prepared to do something stupid.

The gunfire abruptly ceased, and he heard a shout. "She's awake!"

Then a scream erupted, a long pain-filled one. A glance showed Lochlan that Luna was hamstringing the first attacker. The distraction she provided meant he could sprint at one of the new arrivals, who started firing wildly when she turned her gaze on him. A slug hit her in the thigh, and she bared her teeth just as Lochlan tackled the guy to the ground.

A few punches, and the fellow passed out cold. Given the gurgles behind him, Luna was taking care of the fourth assailant, so Lochlan took a minute to strip his fellow of his pants and shirt. They fit a little snugger than he liked, but that was better than running through the woods with his dick bouncing. The shoes, though, were a lost cause. Who the fuck wore a tiny size thirteen?

When Lochlan finally stood in his ill-fitting ensemble, it was in time to see Luna standing over a body, swaying as exhaustion tried to drag her back down.

The drug finally released its hold on her. Her beast shrank, and the fur vanished until only a naked human woman remained, her flesh free of any marks. Strange, given he knew she'd sustained at least one bullet wound.

She blinked at him as she wavered on her feet and slurred, "Is that the last of the hunters?"

"The hunters are long dead. Those guys claimed they were from the Lykosium."

"So it's true," she whispered with a haunted expression. "It's happening."

"What's happening?"

"No time. I must leave before they catch me."

"Why would the Lykosium be after you? Did you do something?"

She didn't reply as she began walking, only to stumble and fall. She hit the ground hard and tried to rise.

"Let me help you." He scooped her up in his arms. Her head lolled against his shoulder.

He thought she was unconscious until she said, "Thank you for saving my life."

"You did most of the killing." He'd merely been a bystander.

She snorted. "You mean the monster did." A strange way to refer to herself.

Rather than return to the lodge they'd escaped, he headed for the SUV they'd parked in the woods, thinking themselves discreet. Upon arriving, he said, "Let's find you some clothes."

Because a naked Luna was massively distracting.

While Luna struggled to put on a shirt, he located his stash of belongings. Lochlan grabbed only his shoes rather than change out of the dead man's clothes. He'd keep his clean stuff for after he'd had a shower.

Ready, he found Luna tangled up in the sleeves of her shirt, leaning against the SUV as if it were the only thing keeping her upright.

"Let me help you."

"I don't need help." She yanked away and almost fell over.

Rather than remark on her idiocy, he grabbed hold of her and helped her free her arms and then poke her head through the neck hole.

This time, she didn't thank him. Hell, she could barely hold her head up, and her eyes were mere slits.

"Sit down while I find you some bottoms."

"I can find them myself." Shaking and pale, Luna rummaged through her bag in the cargo area of the SUV, and he shook his head at her stubborn refusal to admit she wasn't okay.

"You need to rest. The drug Gerard dosed you with has left you weaker than a newborn."

"No time to rest. I have to go. Now." A vehement exclamation at odds with her knees buckling.

Once more, he caught her. "You aren't in any condition to drive. Let's find your son." Because once

Lochlan dumped Luna on Kit, he could wash his hands of her.

"No! I have to stay away from Kit. From everyone. It's safer that way."

As she jangled the keys for the truck, he blurted out, "You're just going to run away? What about Kit?"

"I'll leave a note." She managed to quell her tremors long enough to scribble on a piece of paper torn from a notepad in her bag. The message was simple and concise.

Don't trust the Jawas. Back soon.

"What the fuck is that supposed to mean?"

"He knows who the Jawas are."

"That's it? Not going to explain?"

"Kit will understand. It won't be the first time I've taken off and gone silent." She almost fell over closing the hatch of the SUV.

When she showed her intent to get behind the steering wheel, he drawled, "You're in no condition to drive. I wager you won't make it two miles down the road before crashing."

"I'm stronger than you think."

He had no doubt of that, but even the strongest person had limits. "I'm coming with you."

"Absolutely not," she insisted, the last thing she said before her eyes rolled back and she passed out.

Fuck.

Lochlan had a choice in that moment. He could find the rest of the gang and wash his hands of Luna by handing her over to Kit. Or... Remembering the attack in the woods and Luna's fear, a fear he'd wager she rarely showed, he ended up driving off with a half-naked woman in the back seat.

FOUR

She woke in the back seat of a car, head pounding, mouth feeling pasty.

Pushing up, she noticed the driver had a rugged profile, his hair salt-and-pepper, like his beard. He seemed familiar even as she couldn't place him.

"Who are you? Where are you taking me?" she asked, putting a hand to her brow for a rub.

The man flicked a gaze at her in the rearview. "About time you woke."

"Who are you? For that matter, who am I?"

"You shouldn't drink if you're going to black out."

"I was drinking?" That sounded wrong. She would have sworn she never overindulged.

"We both were after the wedding."

"What wedding?"

His grim reply? "Ours."

She blinked, swallowed, and sat up. "You're my husband?" That couldn't be true.

"Even got the bite to prove it." He angled his head to show the clear mark on his neck left by teeth.

"I did that?" Incredulity pitched the query into the high notes.

"Yup."

"And did we..." Because a bite wasn't what truly caused a pair to be mated. It took sex to cement the chemical bond. Given she wore only a shirt and nothing else but a blanket tucked over her, it seemed likely they'd fucked. But shouldn't she remember? *Please don't let me be mated to a man terrible at sex.*

"I'm hurt, sweetheart. You told me I was the best you've ever had."

Her lips twisted. "Maybe I was being kind."

"As you were biting and clawing me during your climax?"

Her mouth rounded. That really didn't sound like her. And how was it she couldn't remember a thing? "Exactly how much did I drink?"

"You didn't. You were drugged."

The admission had her leaning away from him. "Who are you, and what have you done to me?"

He snorted. "Calm down, sweetheart. Wasn't me who did it. The only thing I'm guilty of is fucking with you for shits and giggles."

"What?" She blinked.

"We're not married."

"I'm so confused. Who are you? Who am I?" She rubbed her forehead to try to ease the ache in her head.

"I'm Lochlan, member of the Feral Pack situated in Northern Alberta, and you're—"

"Luna Smith," she murmured as her memories sluggishly returned, along with the last clear recollection she had of Gerard blowing dust in her face. "That bastard did something to me."

"Yup. Fucker had a chemical compound that forced you to shift into some kind of hybrid wolf beast."

"What?" Her mouth went drier still. It couldn't be. It had been decades since...

"You turned into wolfwoman and went on a seriously epic rampage through the woods. Judging by the look on your face, you don't remember."

She shook her head. "Not really, just bits and pieces." Flashes of red, screams. "What happened?"

"For starters, you single-handedly took out the asshole's army."

That explained the copper taste still in her mouth, while the shifting explained her partial nudity. She tugged the blanket closer over her bare legs. "Were there any casualties on our side?"

"Dunno. You made us leave before checking in with anyone."

"What? I would never do that. Not without checking on Kit."

"You insisted. Left him a note that said, 'Don't trust the Jawas,' which makes no sense because the only Jawas I know are in the *Star Wars* movies."

"It's a code thing between me and Kit." He knew it stood for the Lykosium Council. As a young boy, he'd given them the nickname. In his defense, they did kind of look like the *Star Wars* creatures, given the council wore hooded robes. And some of them did have glowing eyes. "Did I say anything else in the note?"

"'Back soon.' Which was pretty fucking vague if you ask me."

"I agree. We should go back and ensure Kit and the others don't need our help."

"Everyone is fine. Amarok and I traded a few messages before I tossed my phone. He said everyone escaped, including those we found imprisoned in

Gerard's basement. Fucker was going to sell them to his friends as pets."

She remembered the stink of fear and desperation in that basement. Even without the drug she'd have killed Gerard's guards. "Is he dead?"

"Yes. He and the other bodies were tossed into the house before Amarok set it on fire to wipe out all evidence."

Quick thinking by the Alpha of the Feral Pack. "While a fire is good, a cleanup team should still be called in, and the Lykosium will want a report."

"About the council..." Lochlan drummed his fingers on the wheel. "Is there a reason why the Lykosium would want to arrest you?"

Her mouth rounded. "What makes you ask?"

"Because a militia group in the woods demanded I hand you over."

Her stomach clenched. "What makes you think they were Lykosium?"

"It's what they claimed. Said they had orders to bring you in."

"I take it you refused to obey."

"Something about it didn't seem right."

"A good thing, because you likely saved my life." Then she added more softly, "Thank you."

"Bah. I didn't like their tone." He played down

the fact he'd gone against the ruling body of the Were. The Lykosium weren't to be trifled with under normal circumstances.

"I take it the encounter with the Lykosium people is why we're not with the others?"

"We're not with the others because, before you passed out, you told me that you had to get away from everyone. Something about being in danger."

She offered a broken chuckle. "A danger that now includes you, as they'll think you're my accomplice."

"Accomplice to what?"

"Being an arbiter of the truth." Before he could ask, she explained, "There is something rotten in the Lykosium. I've suspected it for some time, but hoped I was wrong." She'd had nothing but a nagging feeling that she hadn't even shared with her son. She'd hoped to chalk it up to paranoia in her old age.

"I take it something has changed?" he queried.

"Yes. That situation with Gerard? It's my belief someone fed him information and covered up his crimes. Kit happened to stumble across them and began to investigate. Despite my precautions, the traitor must have found out and warned Gerard we were coming."

"That would explain the ambush."

"An ambush I should have predicted." She blamed herself. Knowing they had a traitor in their midst, she should have tried to dissuade Kit from investigating the recent decimation of a Pack by unknown causes. As if that would have stopped Kit. He'd tenaciously insisted, while she'd downplayed his findings to the council because she'd suspected there was a spy. She'd been right, and they'd almost paid the price.

"Do you have any proof of a mole?" Lochlan asked.

She shook her head. "No. Just a gut feeling and things that don't add up. For example, you know Kit was investigating some cases of Packs that started losing members more rapidly than accidents, natural deaths, and attrition could account for. Turns out those who went missing were being taken and hunted for sport, the most heinous of crimes. And it should have never happened. We should have been alerted, as the disappearances showed a disturbing pattern."

"Someone covered them up."

She nodded. "Which indicates subterfuge at a high level."

"And that person knows you're on to them, which is why they sent a team after you."

"Mostly likely. With me dead, the traitor might be able to keep his secret."

"So you believe Gerard and his claim it was Kit's father?" He referenced what the human hunter told them. Something to the effect Kit's father had betrayed his own family, that he'd never died and actually worked for the Lykosium. She hated to think someone in charge of protecting the Were and other special folk was involved in such a heinous plot. Then again, this would be the same man who'd effectively handed his family over to a murderer to save himself.

"I don't know what to believe any more than someone wants me gone."

"Gone maybe but not dead."

"What do you mean?"

"They could have shot us dead at any time. You were hanging over my shoulder like a side of beef. They only started shooting—at me, I should add—once I refused to cooperate."

"I thought you said they shot me?"

"In the leg. Through and through. Hardly a fatal wound. They wanted you alive."

"It's not good that they came after me so blatant-ly," she muttered as she gnawed on the tip of her thumb.

"No shit. Now that you're awake, it might be time to ask, what's the plan?"

"I drop you off, and you go home."

He snorted. "You're funny."

"I'm not joking."

"And I'm not leaving."

She tried to digest her pleasure at his refusal to leave. She didn't need his help. At the same time, it would be nice to not be alone. "You'll be in danger if you stick with me."

"Whatever. I'm gonna ask again, what's the plan? Where are we going?"

"I don't know." She honestly didn't. She couldn't trust the Lykosium, only Kit, and until she knew more, she wouldn't endanger him.

"We can't just keep driving. We'll need fuel and food at some point. Not to mention, if I get pulled over, cops are gonna wonder at the half-naked broad riding with me."

"That's easily fixed. My bag is in the back."

"Way to ruin my hope that you'd pretend I'm just so damned hot you had to take off your clothes."

She snorted. "That might sound plausible in the porn you watch, but in the real world, women my age usually wear layers we can peel off in case of a hot flash."

He grinned. "So long as you're sweaty, I think a cop would believe me."

"There is something wrong with you," she grumbled as she leaned over the back seat, looking for her bag.

"Don't suppose you got anything back there to eat? I am starved."

Such a man thing to say, but it was true of her too. Her stomach complained as if she'd not had any sustenance in days. "No food, I'm afraid. We'll need to stop for provisions."

"Easy enough to do. Do you have cash? A credit card can be traced."

"I'm aware. I have a little bit of money to tide us over. If we can get to a town, I can make arrangements for more."

"What kind of arrangements? Because if the Lykosium are looking for you, then I imagine they'll be monitoring your contacts and finances."

His suspicious nature explained why he'd tossed his cell phone. She eyed her bag where her own cell was buried. Only a few people had her number, but just in case... She dragged the bag over the seat for a rummage.

He cleared his throat. "Guess now's a good time to mention I pulled the SIM card and battery out of your cell phone. Figured that was as safe as I could make it."

"Why didn't you do the same to yours?"

His smile proved lopsided as he said, "Popped the SIM, but couldn't peel the back off to remove the battery. So I took the easy way out and destroyed it. Don't feel bad. Can't stand the thing. I only had it because Amarok insisted everyone in the Pack get one."

"It was smart thinking." She no longer knew who she could trust—other than Kit, obviously. And she didn't know enough about Lochlan to trust him. However, given the situation, he was the only person she could rely on at the moment.

"Will your Pack be worried that you didn't rejoin them?" she asked.

"I sent Amarok a quick text before I got rid of my cell. Said I was okay and I'd be in contact soon."

"And you think he'll accept that?"

"Amarok, yes. The others? I'm sure they'll have issues with my disappearance. Ain't much they can do about it, though. I'll explain when I return."

"We can't have them sniffing for us. You might have to contact them and provide a cover story in case the Lykosium question them."

"You think they'll come after my Pack?" he asked sharply.

She shrugged. "I don't know what they'll do. A week ago, I would have said they'd never do something so heinous as aid a murderer or come after me."

"Well, ain't that just fucking peachy?" he grumbled.

"It's not too late for you to escape this mess. I can drop you off at the next town so you can return to your Pack."

He snorted. "I ain't a coward, sweetheart. If something is rotten high up, then going home ain't gonna fix it."

"I don't know if we can fix it."

"Only one way to find out."

"Why are you helping me?" she blurted out. "You barely know me. You don't even like me."

They'd been at odds since meeting. In her case, because of her instant attraction. The man sitting in the driver's seat was her mate. She knew that but would never act upon it. With the secret she carried inside, she had no choice. Lochlan had seen that secret and had not really remarked on it. Perhaps he assumed her monstrous other side was because of the powder Gerard had used on her. Little did he know that monster was a permanent part of her.

"Doing the right thing never needs a reason," he stated.

"I didn't take you for a hero."

He gave a rueful chuckle. "Not a hero, sweetheart. Nor a good guy. And honestly, I know the smart thing would be to walk away."

"But you haven't." Even when she'd been vulnerable.

"Nope. And fuck if I know why."

She did. Because she felt it too. Had circumstances been different, maybe they would have explored the fact they were mates.

FIVE

Luna fell silent, and he thought she'd gone to sleep. Then she said, "You're bleeding."

The wound he'd sustained hurt, but he'd gone through worse. "Yup."

"Stop the car."

"We're in the middle of nowhere."

"Perfect. No one to hear you scream as I take care of your injury."

He snorted. "I'm not a weakling." And yet, he pulled over.

They both piled out of the car with her snapping, "Take off your shirt."

"You're bossy."

"I know. Why do you think they put me on the

council?" she asked, rummaging through the cargo area of the SUV.

"How did you end up working for them?" He knew nothing of the selection process that made someone a Lykosium member.

"I started out as an enforcer."

"They recruited you?"

"You might say that."

A vague reply that he'd wager downplayed something complicated.

Luna emerged with a small sewing kit—and wearing pants. Pity. He'd rather enjoyed seeing her in just a shirt that hit her high on the thigh.

Not exactly the thought he should be having, since a) she was right, they didn't like each other; b) he shouldn't be eyeballing her, given the situation; and c) she might be right about his shoulder needing some help. He'd lost a lot of blood.

His shirt didn't come off easily and required him peeling it away in spots. Only the tug as he tore it from his wound caused a grimace. The bleeding began anew, sluggish and gross. He tossed the soiled shirt in the woods and leaned against the car as she neared with a threaded needle.

"Let's see that wound."

"It's just a little hole. Bullet went right through and didn't hit any bones."

"'Tis but a flesh wound," she badly quoted.

He arched a brow. "Monty Python fan?"

"You sound surprised," she remarked as she poured a bottle of lukewarm water over the gash.

He didn't hiss despite the discomfort. "You don't seem the type."

"And what type am I?"

"The kind who likes foreign movies with subtitles."

At his erroneous assumption, she laughed. "You'd be very wrong. Kit's favorite movie growing up was *Highlander*."

"There can be only one." His turn to quote.

"You've seen it."

"Like a hundred times. It's a classic. As the young pups in the Pack would say, I'm showing my age."

Her lips quirked. "More like showing good taste. Our era did see some of the best movies and music."

"But we're also responsible for boy bands."

"Don't remind me," she groaned. While they conversed, she'd examined his wound. "This is going to hurt," she warned as she put the needle tip against his skin.

"I know." Not the first time he'd needed stitching.

"I'll bet you do," she muttered, most likely because she'd noticed his old scars. More than a few. While Were healed better than most, even they had limits.

But she didn't.

"Do you remember the Lykosium squad shooting you?" he asked, more to distract himself from what she was doing than because he expected a reply.

"No, and I guess they're shit shots, since I'm not injured."

"They didn't miss. I saw you get hit." He waited.

She never paused in her stitching. "Perhaps you were mistaken."

"I'm not."

She said nothing as she continued to tug the hole closed with her dark thread.

"Well?" he prodded.

"Well what?"

"You healed rather quickly, don't you think?"

"If you say so," was her blasé reply.

He sighed. "Is this how it's going to be?"

"What's that supposed to mean?"

"Stop bullshitting me. I'm aware you're not like other Were."

She paused before softly saying, "No, I'm not."

"Gonna explain?"

"Nope." She tied off the last stitch and started putting away her supplies. "And before you ask, let's make it clear right now—we are not discussing the monster."

"Is the rapid healing why the council is after you?" Special powers always drew the wrong kind of attention.

She whirled from the back of the SUV where she'd stowed her sewing kit. Her eyes swirled with annoyance. "You're full of questions."

"Just trying to understand."

"How about you answer some, then? Like why did you stick with me in the woods?"

"Your wolf knows how to have a good time."

"You intentionally put yourself in danger."

"Not really. Though you are pretty vicious when you put your muzzle to it."

"This isn't humorous." She pointed. "You insist on helping me. Why?"

He shrugged. "Dunno." A lie. He'd stuck with her because, like it or not, he was drawn to her. He couldn't walk away. Not then nor now and, frighteningly enough, maybe not ever. The only hope he clung to was she didn't appear interested in keeping him around. If she could remain strong against the mating instinct, then maybe they each stood a chance of staying single.

She wouldn't let it go. "Most people would have tried to save themselves, not put themselves in more danger."

"I'm not most people."

"No shit," she muttered. "We should get moving." She went to the driver side of the SUV, and as she seated herself, she gave him a daring glare. "I'm driving. Don't you dare argue or pull some misogynistic bullshit about how I can't."

He grinned. "I'd never dream of it, sweetheart."

"Don't call me sweetheart. I have a name."

"I know. Problem is, I can't use it."

"Why not?" she asked as he pulled a fresh shirt from his knapsack, despite the fact he still needed a shower.

"Used to have a pet hamster called Luna."

She blinked at him. "You had a hamster with my name?"

"Yup. And while you're many things, a cute little cuddly furball ain't one of them."

Her lips thinned. "Oh, then what am I?"

He could have given her some bullshit reply that

would have pleased her strong personality. But he was still a man, a man who'd gotten a boner the first time he'd seen her.

So what came out of his mouth instead was, "A hot vixen."

would have pleased her strong personality. For he
was still a man whom when got on a horse the first
time held such her.

So what came out of his mouth instead was, "A
hot vixen."

SIX

IT DIDN'T HAPPEN OFTEN THAT LUNA WAS AT A
loss for words. Also new? Her silence came with
heated cheeks. All because he'd complimented her.

And Lochlan noticed. He chuckled softly. "Let
me guess. You don't like being called a hot vixen
either."

"That's the word for a female fox."

"Exactly. Since you're the mother of a fox, I'd say
that totally makes you a sexy vixen."

The blush came on even stronger, but she
managed to exclaim, "Now is neither the time nor
place for you to be hitting on me."

"I disagree. We're alone on a long road trip. Can't
imagine a better time to flirt. Let's be honest, we're
attracted to each other."

"Ha." She snorted.

"No point in denying it. And it's understandable. I am considered handsome, and if it makes you feel better, my hot vixen, I've been called a silver fox more than once."

"Enough. I will not just sit here and let you proposition me as if I'm a hooker for hire. I'm not interested in sex with you."

"You are."

"Am not!" she huffed, digging the lying ditch even deeper.

He chuckled. "Okay, sweetheart. Whatever you say."

"Your levity isn't appreciated."

"Maybe you should lighten up."

"Excuse me? I don't think you get to say how I am allowed to act."

"True, I don't, but I will say I've heard about you. A woman who is tough as nails. You'd have to be if you're on the Lykosium Council."

"Exactly. You should show me respect."

"Not sure where the disrespect is."

"Your comments are highly inappropriate."

"Says you. I see it as complimenting someone where it's due."

"I'd rather you didn't."

"Trust me, I wish my fucking mouth would stop spouting off, too, but apparently, where you're concerned, I've got a wayward tongue."

The mention of his tongue had her eyeing his mouth then quickly looking away before he caught her. "What's that supposed to mean?"

"We really gonna pretend, sweetheart? I know you feel it. The mating need." She opened her mouth to refute that, but he kept talking. "And before you lie, I know you are because I'm fighting it too."

"Fighting it?"

"Let's be honest, both of us are too old to settle down."

"We are." She'd said that so many times when Kit had asked her why she remained single.

"I'm ornery, you're bossy, it would never work."

"No shit," she muttered, even as she enjoyed their repartee.

"I've seen and done shit that I can't talk about. But trust me when I say, I'm not mate material."

"Me either," was her soft whisper.

"Then we're agreed? No mating."

"Never. And no flirting."

"I guess that would be playing with fire. Fine. You win. I'll be a perfect gentleman. Wake me when it's my turn to drive."

The strange conversation set down some boundaries that should have pleased her. She didn't want to be mated. So why was she insulted when he admitted he didn't want it either?

Because she enjoyed the flirting even as she knew it would lead to touching, stroking, and kissing and sex and claiming.

I have to be strong.

When it was his turn to drive, she faked sleep only to hide within the hood of her sweatshirt while she stared out the window. They'd been driving for almost four hours, only barely stopping for gas paid in cash. The day dawned overcast and gray. A thick forest flanked both sides of the road, and only the lines strung between poles showed they'd not completely abandoned civilization.

"Where are we?" she asked, pretending to wake.

"Middle of nowhere."

"Not exactly an answer."

"Been taking the back roads since I wasn't sure just how many agencies the Lykosium might have a hand in. Guess now that you're awake, you can answer some questions. Do we have to worry about the cops looking for us? Can they create a fake arrest warrant or tap police agency scanners and shit?"

"Not likely." She shook her head then bit her lip.

"Then again, maybe? I really don't know what to expect or how deep the traitor's influence goes."

"I'd say pretty far, given what they managed to hide. I also get the impression he's readying to make his big move."

"What makes you say that?" She turned to eye him, finding his strong profile appealing. His jawline was covered in a soft burr of hair.

"The fact they blatantly came after you."

The reminder rendered her silent because he'd pinpointed her dilemma. By acting, the traitor had revealed his existence, turning suspicion to reality. At the same time, the traitor's very actions made it appear as if he didn't fear retaliation. That suggested the traitor, who, according to Gerard, was Kit's own father—insanity if true—was placed highly enough on the council to avoid punishment.

Who was it, though? Until now, she'd thought she knew her fellow council members well, or as well as was possible for the secretive group. Some never took down their hoods when they met. As for scent, Kit was young when she found him, and she'd never met his father, meaning they had no scent or even an image to go by.

"You're thinking awfully hard," Lochlan remarked.

"Debating how much I can tell you." Could she tell him the honest truth, which was not something she indulged in too often? As part of the Lykosium Council, she kept secrets. So many secrets. Perhaps that was part of the problem. Transparency would have exposed the problem sooner.

"Ah, yes, because I'm the one you can't trust," he drawled.

"I've yet to figure out your true motive for rescuing me from those woods and leaving your Pack on a whim."

"Maybe you were right and I wanted to be a hero for a day."

She snorted. "You're too cynical for that."

That brought another curve to his lips. "I think I've been pegged. Fact remains, as tempted as I was to ditch your ass, you were in no condition to drive."

"By aiding me, you've painted a target on yourself."

"I already had one. I'm more worried about my Pack. Will the Lykosium go after them?"

Her lips flattened. "I don't know. My guess is they'll probably try to surveil Kit to see if he'll lead them to me."

"Try?"

Her turn to smirk. "My son isn't easy to spy on.

He knows how to disappear. He'll spot any watchers easily enough and ensure they don't learn anything." Knowing him, he'd spirit Poppy away to his secret house of lost children. Apparently, Luna's adoption of a lonely boy was hereditary. Her son had a habit of rescuing young Were people in need.

"What of the others?"

"Your Pack should be fine, as they aren't associated with me."

"You just went on a mission with them."

"A single failed mission whereupon I disappeared and they went home. That should be enough to keep them safe."

"Unless I suddenly show up," Lochlan pointed out. "If the traitor suspects I abetted you, then going home is probably the worst thing I could do."

"I agree." More softly, she added, "Sorry."

"Don't be. You tried to convince me to walk away."

And he hadn't. Not yet. That deserved something from her. "Thank you for not listening. I don't know if I'd have made it this far without you."

"Somehow, I doubt that. You're one tough lady."

"Tough, yes, but even I need to admit I could use some help," she said with a sigh. She hated feeling weak. And now was not the time to let pride stand in the way of doing the right thing.

"If you need help, then you've got the wrong man. You should have asked the boys in my Pack, then. Last thing you need is an old wolf like me fighting a young pups' battle."

"You're not old." A quick glance sideways showed he'd quirked his lips.

"We're both well aware of my age."

"I prefer to refer to our advanced years of experience as seasoning." Lochlan was a man who'd seen things. It made him sexier. "Exactly how old are you?"

"Didn't your file on me say?" he mocked.

"Actually, I know very little about you." She'd not had the time to dig any deeper into the man before events had snowballed.

"As it should be."

"What's that supposed to mean?"

"I've been doing my best to not leave any trace."

"Why? Did you commit a crime in your past?"

His jaw tensed. "Not exactly."

"That's not an answer."

"You're right, it's not. But I will say it's part of the reason I stuck around when shit went down with you."

"You're not making any sense."

He sighed. "I know. So I'm going to be blunt. The powder that gave you no choice but to shift? I've seen it before."

The stark, low tone gave her a chill as she whispered, "Where?"

"When I was in the military."

SEVEN

LUNA WENT QUIET AFTER HIS ANNOUNCEMENT and stared ahead at the road that would take them from a two-lane country highway onto a larger thoroughfare that would lead to an interstate.

When she remained silent, he cleared his throat. "I'm gonna take a wild guess and say you didn't realize the military knows about us."

"No." A low admission.

"If it helps, I'm pretty sure it's not common knowledge. The Were troops they conscript are kept apart from others."

"No, that doesn't help," she growled. She turned her head toward him enough that he could see her eyes swirl with a storm of colors. "How did they find out about our existence? Someone must have blabbed."

"Not necessarily. They might have noticed something during the extensive bloodwork they do when we enlist."

She shook her head. "Doubtful. Our DNA is the same as everyone else's. The difference appears to come from up here." She tapped her temple. "Those who are Were have a mental switch that allows them to change shape."

"Then I don't know how they found out. It ain't as if I wrote 'turns furry' on the full moon on my application," was his sarcastic rejoinder.

"How did you come to be in the military?"

"Lack of prospects. Joined at eighteen to get out of my small town. Deployed a few times before they recruited my ass for a special detachment."

"And you didn't think to question the fact they knew about your shifting ability?" she asked flatly.

"I was a dumbass in his twenties. One day, Sergeant McLean, who was a Were, pulled me out of the barracks and asked if I'd like to be reassigned to a special unit. Claimed it was Lykosium-sanctioned."

"And you took him at his word?"

"Why wouldn't I? It's not as if the Lykosium are exactly transparent in their dealings."

Her lips pursed. "The secrecy is to protect the Were."

"Yeah, well, that same protection is also a hindrance, because I didn't know any better. The sergeant made it sound like I'd be doing something important for the Lykosium. I had no reason to disbelieve him."

"When you say 'unit,' how many soldiers are we talking about?"

"The number varied. The most we ever had was eight. After a really bad mission, that dropped to three before they brought in some new blood."

Hearing that some of them had died brought a wince to her expression. "You mentioned the sergeant who recruited you being Were. What of the commanding officer?"

"Human. And before you ask, he knew exactly what we were. Everyone working with us did, about a half-dozen humans, all told."

"Which is a half dozen too many."

"Yeah, but at the same time, like I said, we were a closely kept secret."

She went silent for a moment before asking, "You indicated you have some experience with the powder that forced me to shift."

"Yup. Well, variations of it, at any rate. When

the human colonel in charge wasn't dropping us in the field for a mission, the military had a team of scientists who liked to try serums and shit on us."

That widened her eyes. "You're talking of experimentation. On people."

"Yup."

"And you allowed it?" Her query had an incredulous note.

"None of us wanted it. We didn't have a fucking choice," he growled. "They dropped us into hostile situations as cannon fodder, and when we weren't risking our lives, they used us for wolf-pig experiments."

"Testing what?"

"How fast we could heal. What kind of poison we could metabolize and still remain functional. The forced shift was another one. Their quest was to find a way to make us stronger, fiercer. One doctor in particular was working on a way to make us into wolfmen."

"I'm afraid to ask what that means."

"They wanted us to maintain the human ability to problem-solve after we shifted. They wanted us to have claws to fight but fingers with fine motor skills. Wolves suck at opening doors or stealing hard drives. Not to mention, wolves can't exactly climb walls."

"Did they succeed?" she asked.

"No. Many of their failures led to death. A half-shifted Were is in constant pain."

"Sounds horrible."

"No shit," was his gruff reply. He didn't want or need her pity.

"Did you try to escape?"

"To ensure our compliance, they implanted us with trackers in different spots so we wouldn't know where to slice to remove them. If someone ran, a signal could be sent at the press of a button that caused them to go into an instant coma until they were retrieved."

"Damn," she whispered. "How did you get away?"

"Not easily," was his wry response. "The military thinks I died in a helicopter crash. It was a close call. We got shot down." His simple reply didn't tell of the terror he'd felt as they were hit, the smoke billowing so thick he couldn't see, but he could feel the whirly-bird spinning out of control. The memory of the impact sometimes still jarred him awake. "I was the only survivor, but I sustained heavy injuries. A gash in my thigh revealed the implant. After I popped the tracker out, I blew up the wreckage by tossing a grenade at the gas tank."

"The military didn't hunt for survivors?"

"I'm sure they tried, but I didn't stick around to find out. I covered my tracks and disappeared."

She rubbed her lower lip. "That explains why the Lykosium file on you is sparse."

"That's because I borrowed the identity of Lochlan McGuire from a dead human." He changed the subject. "There's a town coming up in five miles. You sure you want us to stop?"

She nodded. "We need to regroup and replenish."

"We should be ditching this SUV in case those tracking you have the cops looking for it."

"I paid cash for it and used a false identity."

"And yet, they still found you at Gerard's hunting property."

"Because they knew Kit was taken and that I'd go looking for him."

"Or they're tracking you."

At the suggestion, she shook her head wildly. "I am not chipped."

"You're not, and yet, Kit, your son, is?" He didn't mask his incredulity, because it seemed unlikely that she wasn't also chipped, given they'd just used the tracker in her son to find him.

"Blame my overprotective nature for his tracker.

Given my role on the Lykosium Council, I don't have a tracker. None of the council members do."

"If you say so."

Her lips thinned. "I'd know if I carried a foreign object in my body."

The statement came from hope and emotion, not fact. He refrained from replying, because she wouldn't like what he had to say.

She guessed it anyhow and snapped, "You think I'm wrong."

"I think we'll find out soon enough." Because if she was being tracked, another attack would happen. And soon.

EIGHT

Given Lochlan looked more or less presentable, if scruffy, he volunteered to be the one to rent them a room using the cash she had on hand. She'd brought a good amount on the rescue mission, as if she'd known she might have to go off-grid. Lochlan didn't ask, and she didn't let him know exactly how much she had. People could get weird when it came to money. While Lochlan didn't give off a thieving vibe, she thought it best to keep her cards—and dollar bills—close to her chest.

Could she trust him?

Mate.

Her primal side didn't feel the same qualms. She chose to ignore it and focus on something other than the handsome man walking into the motel office. The man who'd saved her.

It still stunned Luna that she'd been so brazenly attacked by the traitor and his minions. He must have been getting worried she'd figure out his identity. Pity she still had no idea who that was. Although, if she went by people she didn't like who served on or around the Lykosium Council, that narrowed the traitor's identity down to only about a dozen.

If she'd died, what she'd discovered would have died with her. Maybe she should let someone know of her suspicions. But who? If she said anything to Kit, he'd do something foolish, like go after the culprit. He could get hurt.

It was up to her to stop the traitor, but maybe she didn't have to do it alone.

Lochlan already knew about the rot within the Lykosium. Parts of it at least. In a shocking twist, he'd revealed things she hadn't known, such as the military being aware of the existence of the Were. How was that possible? The council should have known of such a breach but didn't. Could it be the traitor hid the evidence?

Not for long. If Luna managed one more thing in

this life, it would be to expose the person behind the decimation and cruelty to her people.

The traitor would die.

Lochlan emerged from the motel office. Anyone watching would have seen a man at ease, partially slouched, eyes down as he watched his steps, hands shoved in his pockets. The reality? Lochlan studied everything around him, relying on his auditory and olfactory senses, plus that one thing not everyone knew how to use—instinct.

As he neared their vehicle, a part of her understood that the reason he suddenly smiled and waved was in case anyone watched. They were a happy couple, not a pair of wanted Were trying to avoid notice.

She smiled back and kept the smile on her face as he slid into the vehicle. "What are the room numbers?"

"One room. Second floor." He drove around to the middle of the motel.

She noted his odd choice of room location. "I'd have thought you'd want a ground-level corner unit for an easier escape."

"Much easier to pen us in too. No, thanks. Being on a different level gives us warning, because no matter what, they're coming up the stairs."

"Or landing on the roof."

"Wrong kind of roof and we'd hear the helicopter long before it arrived. Not to mention they're not sending a helicopter. We're talking covert ops. If anyone comes after us, it will be in full gear—night-vision goggles, climbing apparatus, full drone support. I also predict a power failure."

"The Lykosium don't have that kind of equipment or organization. You've met our enforcers."

"And I met the group in the woods. They had guns. Armor. They came prepared."

Could he be exaggerating? She remembered nothing of those moments. But why would he lie?

"How many beds?" she asked as he parked between two cars.

"Two beds in the room I rented. Not sure about the one we'll be staying in."

She pursed her lips. "Say again?"

"The motel has adjoining rooms and is archaic enough to still use actual keys instead of key cards. When the desk guy wasn't looking, I swiped the key for the room next door."

She glanced upward as they headed up the stairs. "Aren't you being a tad paranoid?"

"Nope."

"What if there's another key and the clerk rents that room?"

"Then there's much laughter and embarrassment as we return to our proper room."

"You've got an answer for everything."

"I wish," he muttered as he stopped in front of room fourteen and slotted the key. "We have to remember when leaving the room to come out of the correct door in case we're being watched."

"You still think I'm chipped."

"I'm being cautious. Something I'd think someone being hunted by the Lykosium would appreciate."

"What I don't appreciate is the way you think you're in charge and making the decisions."

He arched a brow. "I rented a room, which you agreed with."

"And you stole a key."

"Because it would have been dumb not to. Listen, if you don't like it, then you can stay in the official room, and I'll sleep next door. Probably better that way. I'll bet you snore."

Her jaw dropped. "Do not."

"How would you know?"

"Because I do."

"Whatever, sweetheart."

"My name is Luna."

"It's like you want me to think of you as a furry, warm pet." His gaze dipped, and her cheeks heated fiercely.

"Is there a reason you're trying to goad me?"

"Because it's fun," he replied as he shut their motel door, encasing them in a room she'd seen a hundred times on a hundred trips.

Two queen-sized beds topped with floral comforters, the rough-and-tough fabric kind. Pillows covered in white, bleached slipcovers. Furniture made of thick wood, dented and scarred from years of abuse. The carpet a medley of swirling colors excellent at hiding stains.

The television appeared to be the only upgrade. The flat-screen was mounted on the wall, the remote attached to a chain bolted to a ring secured to the wall by the nightstand. Classy.

Still, the idea of a hot shower and a bed sounded heavenly.

Lochlan went to the door separating them from room thirteen and unlocked their side, only to be confronted by the flat expanse of the panel on the other side. No keyhole to unlock.

"I think your plan's a bust," she said.

"Oh, ye of little faith. You seem to think this is

my first rodeo, sweetheart. We'll get inside. Watch and see."

Lochlan pulled out his wallet and a credit card, which he used to wedge between the lock and the jamb. When that didn't work, he tried peeling the trim away to expose the tongue for the door.

"How's it going?" she asked.

He cast her a grin. "Great. One more second." He kicked the door, and it slammed open.

She arched a brow. "So much for subtle."

"If motel management checks their unrented rooms, we're already in trouble."

"The military teach you to break into places?"

He glanced at her. "I lived in a rough neighborhood before I enlisted."

Exactly who was Lochlan McGuire? Because he'd admitted earlier to using a dead man's identity.

"What next, paranoid one?"

"No lights, at all. Or television, for that matter."

"What? No *Survivor* before bed? Just ruin the only joy I had left in my life." She shook her head.

"Better ready than sorry."

The rebuke burned because, for all she thought herself careful, he took his protection to the next level.

"Let's say you're right and they hit." She swept a

hand toward the room next door. "How does it help to be this close? This ensures we can't go out the door without running into them."

"Ideally, we avoid them before they get that far. A few motion-triggered cameras will help with that."

She arched a brow. "Because you happened to pack some?"

"Nope, but they're easy to buy these days and cheap too. I'm going to clean up quick and pop out to buy some."

"I thought we were supposed to stay low."

"It's doubtful they'll hit in the daytime. If they're even on our trail yet. Unless they had another team waiting in the wings, they'll need time for a new group to arrive."

She thought he was overestimating the situation. "Go. I'll be fine without you."

"It won't be long. Motel clerk says there's a strip mall with an electronics place two miles down the road. I'll walk in case you need the car to flee."

Another decision made. By him.

She could have protested his orders, but then he might stay in the room, and she'd have to shower knowing he was nearby. A woman had only so much self-restraint. Being locked in a vehicle with him, smelling him, hour after hour... She needed time away from Lochlan.

"If you're going to go shopping, grab us some clothes, too, and food." She handed over some of her cash.

He eyed the wad of hundred-dollar bills. "This will not be discreet."

"It's harder to carry large amounts of small denominations."

"Maybe you should come with me."

"I'd rather shower."

The simple remark caused his nostrils to flare. "Keep your eyes and especially your ears open. While I doubt anyone would attack during daylight, they might be subtle about it."

"You worry too much, papa wolf."

His jaw hitched. "Don't call me that."

"Or what, papa wolf? After all, didn't you call me vixen?"

"You're a mother. I'm nothing."

"You're a man who worries too much about everything."

"Because I know better than to trust. I gotta clean up quick before I go out. I'll use our actual room so you have your privacy." He practically ran into the next room, only to sheepishly return after his shower in a towel.

He indicated the bags by the bed. "Forgot my clean clothes."

She did her best not to stare, keeping her head turned away, but she couldn't hide from his scent. It hit her as ambrosia to the senses. She closed her eyes and inhaled.

"You okay?" he asked.

"Yup. Just fine." Said perhaps a little too brightly. She turned and noticed he'd donned a plaid shirt, jeans and brown leather steel-toed boots.

He raked fingers through his damp hair. "Last chance to join me. Or I can stay."

"I don't need a babysitter. Have fun."

She pulled the heavy wooden dresser across the busted adjoining door after he left before she jumped in the shower, hating that his paranoia had her feeling vulnerable. However, her need to sluice the filth from the battle from her skin won over any worry about being interrupted. She gargled with water and spit over and over, but the actions didn't fully rinse the taste of blood from her mouth. It had been a long time since she'd tasted it. The coppery taint hadn't changed.

Despite knowing what she'd see, she eyed herself

in the mirror. Her smooth skin was unblemished by scars or wounds, thanks to an unnatural healing ability that was the result of the experiments done on her. Like Lochlan, she, too, had escaped people who'd conducted experiments on her. Unlike him, she didn't fear being found again, because not one of those involved in her childhood torture remained alive.

When an enforcer named Padme had found her, she'd been covered in blood, wide-eyed and shaking. Padme asked the traumatized teenager what had happened. *The monster got them,* she'd said.

A monster that had disappeared that night, a night in which only one young girl had been rescued from a secret laboratory doing experiments on Were. The Lykosium enforcers had found the buried bodies of Dr. Adams' victims in the yard. Many of them had been misshapen.

When questioned further by those who'd rescued her about what had happened, she'd given a partial truth. *The doctor hurt me.* That reply had seemed answer enough as to why she never shifted after that. Because she didn't want anyone to know of the monster that lurked inside.

A monster Lochlan had seen, along with noting her almost magical ability to heal. Would he tell anyone? If he was half the man she thought he was, no, he wouldn't.

Emerging from the steamy bathroom wrapped in a towel, Luna eyed the motel room with its pair of beds. Rather than the floral patterns of the room next door, the solid forest green comforters barely matched the yellow walls and clashed with the bright blue pillows. The dark low-pile carpet didn't show any overt stains, but she could smell the filth. She didn't want to walk barefoot on it, but she'd left her bag on the bed farthest from the bathroom.

Digging through it, she found what she needed and dressed quickly, wishing she'd packed more than clothes. A weapon would have been nice. In retrospect, she should have gone with Lochlan. She could have bought a few things and shown him that she did know how to survive. She'd been doing it almost her entire life, but she had admittedly become complacent.

Blame her time with the Lykosium. They'd rescued her from a life of torture and experiments. Helped her get right in her head, given her purpose and the skills to forge that purpose. She'd spent more than three decades making Were like herself safe from the evil doctors of the world. She'd hunted down every single person involved in her incarceration. Not one had survived.

Her ruthlessness to the Were cause and keeping of their secret eventually had led to the invitation to sit on the council. An honor at the time, and yet, she missed the days of being an enforcer, of being out in the field, acting rather than reacting and meting out justice.

She fidgeted by the window, remaining discreetly hidden and doing her best to see outside despite the thick curtains.

I hate waiting.

Look at her trying to be patient, not something that came easily, just like trust. Only one person had her back, Kit. Yet here she was, putting her life in the hands of a virtual stranger.

Mate.

She ignored the word in her mind in favor of the cold, hard facts. She didn't know Lochlan, a man who claimed that wasn't even his name.

Who was he? What did she really know about him? What if he worked for the person who wanted her out of the way? What if he contacted the Lykosium and led them to her? Hell, right now, he might be talking to the Alpha of Feral Pack, telling him everything, not realizing someone from the Lykosium might be listening.

If only she could research his past. She itched to log onto the secret Lykosium servers that stored all their files, but doing so would lead directly back to her. She couldn't allow that.

They can't find me.

If they couldn't find Luna, would they go after Kit?

The thought filled her with a motherly rage. He might not be the flesh of her body, but he was the son of her heart, and she'd be damned if she let anyone harm him.

But how could she best protect him?

The answer didn't hit her before Lochlan's return. He came through the door to room fourteen, and she waited for him to close that door before she opened the adjoining one, having already removed the dresser.

"I come bearing gifts," he announced as he entered with a few bags, the one with food interesting her the most. They'd not eaten since their last stop for gas. Chips, protein sticks, and juice weren't a proper meal, not for someone like her who'd expended so much energy to not only shift but also heal.

He'd brought simple fare—several burgers loaded with lettuce, tomato, and condiments; fries and onion rings; even chicken nuggets, which she dipped in the mess that dripped from the burgers she ate.

They said little as they ate, but once the food had disappeared, she leaned back with a sigh. "I needed that."

"No shit. I've never seen a woman pack away that much food in one sitting."

"Our experience left me depleted."

"You should have said something. We could have stopped earlier for a more substantial meal."

"We needed to get as far away as possible."

"I don't think distance will matter. If the traitor wants you, he'll keep sending troops until they find you."

"Maybe. Perhaps he'll rethink it given they lost the perfect opportunity."

"The traitor won't want you running around and talking to people. With his safety on the line, I doubt he'll give up."

She grimaced. "I can't believe we're discussing this. The Lykosium should have been above this kind of thing. Fuck, we're supposed to stop it." She couldn't help but grumble.

"The Lykosium still can." He eyed her as he said it.

He had a point. So long as she tried to expose the traitor, he wouldn't win. "I'm worried he'll try to get to me through Kit. In retrospect, I should have probably dragged him along with me."

"He wouldn't have left Poppy."

"No, he wouldn't have," she agreed softly. Kit had found his mate, and nothing would keep them apart. Luna wanted him to have someone in case things went sideways for her. She eyed Lochlan. "I need to assure his safety. His and everyone else's."

"Meaning you need to expose the traitor."

"Easier said than done. How can I find something that doesn't appear to exist? You're the ex-military man. What would you suggest?"

"Asking a grunt on the ground? I'm not a spy. Usually, I was aimed at the problem and expected to provide a fatal solution."

"That doesn't help me until I have a name." She sighed. "I wish I had access to my computer."

"But you don't. What you do have is your years of service as a council member. You're privy to many of their secrets. You probably interacted with this person a fair bit. Maybe he did or said something."

"Not that I can recall."

He kept trying. "What about hair color? Can't be too many redheads around."

"Kit's mother was the redhead. And fox. Meaning his dad had to be a wolf."

"Mixed-species mating isn't supposed to be possible," Lochlan reminded her.

"Fox shifters are special. Given their low numbers, it seems nature gave them the ability to not just procreate with humans but Were too." She didn't mention the fact that foxes and wolves weren't the only Were out there.

"I don't suppose you keep DNA profiles on the members? Something we can compare with Kit."

She shook her head. "I never suspected any of them of anything until recently. I know these people, for the most part. We've been colleagues for years, fighting for the same thing. While some of them can be jerks, it's hard to imagine any of them doing such a thing as enabling a murderer."

"Maybe it's not someone on the council itself but one of their lackeys."

At that, she rolled her shoulders. "Perhaps. But that's not what Gerard claimed."

"Gonna believe a liar?"

"How do I know if it was a lie?" She sighed. "My head is such a mess it's hard to think straight."

"Then sleep on it. We'll figure out a plan of action in the morning."

"Sleep does sound good." She eyed the bed then said, "Let me guess. You're going to stand watch."

"Yes, but not the way you think. I bought some help." He indicated the plastic bag he'd carried up with the food. "I snagged a few motion cameras." He tore open boxes and plugged them into various outlets.

"Need help installing them?"

He eyed his watch. "They'll need a solid two to three hours to charge enough to last the night. You might as well go to sleep in the meantime. I'll keep watch."

Whatever. She'd done her due diligence and offered.

She expected to have a hard time falling asleep, especially with him in the room, but in no time, she found herself drifting, dreaming and remembering the first time she'd become a monster.

It had ended with everyone being dead.

NINE

LOCHLAN DID HIS BEST TO BE QUIET AS HE activated each camera and linked it to the disposable phone he'd purchased. Not that anything he did disturbed Luna. She quickly fell asleep, facing away from him, her breathing slow and steady.

She'd needed the rest. The dark circles under her eyes attested to her weariness. Just like the amount of food she'd inhaled had showcased how much energy she'd expended. It hadn't occurred to him before that her savage shape, and insanely fast healing, might require more fuel. He'd remember for next time, because he had no doubt they'd gotten away too easily.

Despite her insistence that she wasn't being

tracked, he had to wonder. That was why he'd bought a frequency detector. Hopefully, it would ping if she did indeed bear a tracking device.

He waited until he could be sure she slept deeply before standing over her, passing the scanner back and forth numerous times. Not a single blip.

He tested it on the remote cameras broadcasting a signal. Ping. So it did work. Maybe she was clean. But he'd take no chances.

This late in the autumn season, the sun went down early, and people weren't as likely to be out and about. The moment night fell, he headed outside. For the next part, he couldn't avoid being seen. Then again, he was fine with letting anyone who might be watching know that he waited for them. They might think twice before attacking.

Doubtful. Lochlan knew all about determined people.

Under the guise of having a smoke, Lochlan wandered around and paused in the areas where he wanted to affix cameras. He used the double-sided tape he'd purchased to stick the motion cameras in various spots approaching the room, all of them feeding their images to the cell phone he'd purchased. He'd even stuck his head out the window of the room bathroom and affixed a pair to the wall, one aiming up, the other down. Seven cameras in all. If they spent a quiet night, he'd grab them before they left. He didn't want the almost six hundred dollars they'd cost to go to waste. At least the guy at the counter hadn't even asked him why he needed so many.

Once the security was in place, he placed a call anonymously. No one answered after three rings, so he hung up and waited before dialing anew.

Amarok answered right away but said nothing.

"Did you remember to pasture the cow?" Code for *all is good*.

"Yeah, she kicked me again, though." Meaning *the line is clear*. They could talk freely.

"Got a minute to chat?" Lochlan asked.

"Yup, just give me a second. "

He could hear the sound of a door opening and closing then the noise of a freeway. His Pack Alpha wasn't yet home. He had at least a day or more of driving left.

"Okay, I think we're good. Where are you?" Amarok asked.

"In the middle of bum-fuck." Lochlan rubbed his face, wishing he could say more, but just in case the traitor with the Lykosium had tapped Amarok's phone, he couldn't take a chance.

"You okay? You need me?" Amarok would come if Lochlan asked.

As if Lochlan would be so weak. It was nice knowing the guy cared, though. "I'm good. More than good. Just taking a bit of a scenic route with my lady friend. Figure we'll drive down around the coast, take in the sights, walk barefoot on the beach." Amarok knew how much Lochlan hated sand. But this was about planting a false narrative that would also act as a warning.

"Sounds like fun."

"Yup." He faked enthusiasm and then tried to not sound too raspy as he said, "Gonna miss Poppy's cooking. Her new boyfriend is one lucky bastard." Did Amarok get what Lochlan was trying to say?

"Speaking of her boyfriend," Amarok said, "mind if Poppy and Kit borrow your place while you're gone? Might be a little cramped if they have to share that tiny cabin with her brother."

"Go ahead. For as long as she needs."

"I'll make sure to burn the sheets before you get back."

"Ugh. Don't remind me." Poppy was like a daughter to him. "Make sure he takes care of her."

"Oh, I'll keep a close eye on them, don't you worry."

He almost sighed in relief as Amarok confirmed he understood. Poppy would need watching. As Kit's mate, she might be in danger.

"Don't expect we'll be back for a while."

Amarok said nothing for a second. "Take care. Call if you get stuck anywhere."

"I will." A soft reply.

Amarok lightened the tone with, "About time you took a vacation, you ornery bastard."

"Guess I just needed to find the right woman." The moment he said it, Lochlan wanted to shoot himself. He quickly closed the conversation. "I should go. Gonna get an early start tomorrow so we can make it to some historic park she keeps going on and on about."

"Safe travels, my friend."

"You too," Lochlan muttered before hanging up. It killed him to not be going home with Amarok and the others, especially knowing they might be in danger. However, Luna needed him more than his capable Alpha. Hopefully, if anybody had been listening, they would turn their attention away from the Feral Pack.

Come after me. He'd teach them a lesson they

wouldn't forget. Security in place, he climbed the stairs to his and Luna's room. His arrival pinged his phone with warnings from the cameras that caught his motion. Good to see it was all working. He left the volume of the phone notifications on high.

As he entered the room, he felt his tension ease at the sound of her even breathing. Funny how he'd not realized his anxiety until it was assuaged.

He stripped to his boxers and lay on the bed parallel to hers, comforted by her presence even as he remained too aware of her.

My mate.

The certainty hit him harder each time he came within proximity of her, as if it were a foregone conclusion. A week ago, he would have scoffed at the idea.

Lochlan was an old dog in his late forties, and some would say he was too settled in his ways to ever get hitched. It would take a special kind of woman to accept his grumpy ass. Not to mention his nightmares.

A good thing he didn't plan to sleep. He never did without his pills, and given how they knocked him out, he couldn't risk it, not with the danger stalking them. He knew better than to close his eyes and let the night terrors reign.

Better to stay awake. He'd nap tomorrow while she drove.

That was the plan.

Only he'd not counted on his fatigue. Before he knew it, he slept. As if it'd been waiting in the shadows, the nightmare pounced.

TEN

LUNA WOKE TO A NOISE. A MOAN, TO BE EXACT, and it hadn't come from her. She lay still and listened. Breathed. Smelled Lochlan in the room. Heard him breathing. Then muttering, "Leave me alone."

She could have ignored it. Only she found herself drawn to his bedside. In repose, his features relaxed, and she could stare without qualms at the square line of his jaw, barely visible in the gloomy room. His brow creased as he grimaced in his sleep. The bed creaked as he shifted, and his head turned from side to side. He was a man in the grips of a nightmare.

She reached out to soothe him. The moment her flesh touched his, she was drawn in.

"CORPORAL LOWIN, *fall out and report to the command tent.*"

"Yes, sir."

Lowin did a rigid about-face and marched off, knowing better than to linger or slouch while that hard-ass Lieutenant Murdock was watching. He'd have him doing pushups until his arms were jelly again.

On his way to the command tent, he ran into Lochlan, only recently released from the infirmary and still limping. The shrapnel he'd taken had torn a chunk out of his calf that no amount of medicine—or good genetics—could fix.

"Lochlan, hey, how's it going?" Lowin stopped for a quick chat with the other soldier, one of his few friends in camp.

"It's going." Lochlan shrugged. "Just got my walking papers and flight home."

"You're leaving?"

"Don't got a choice." He thumped his thigh. "Apparently, I'll never be fit for duty, and I am not cut out to be a pencil pusher or a cook."

"Shit. What are you going to do?"

Lochlan shrugged, his thin frame even slimmer

since the accident. Camp food didn't exactly help a guy put on the pounds. "Dunno. Probably become a farmer like my dad wanted."

"My condolences." Lowin knew how much Lochlan hated the idea. It was why the guy had joined in the first place.

Lochlan chuckled. "Guess I should try and find something to like about it since it's the only job I'm good for now."

"Good luck." They shook hands, and Lowin continued to the command tent.

An MP standing outside barked, "What's your business, soldier?"

"I was told to present myself."

"And you are?"

"Corporal Lowin."

The MP glared at him before sticking his head in the tent. "A grunt is here. Says he was told to come, sir. A Corporal Lowin."

"Send him in."

Upon entering, he noticed two people inside. The general, with his balding pate and jowly cheeks. While he was not supposed to smoke in the tent, he had the butt of a cigar clamped between his lips. With him was a younger officer, forties at the most, with a *scent that confused Lowin, mostly because he lacked one.*

Realizing he stared, Lowin straightened his posture, saluted, and set his gaze straight ahead.

"At ease, Corporal," the general commanded.

He tucked his hands behind his back.

"I called you in to meet Colonel Mayflower."

He quickly saluted.

"Colonel Mayflower has been tasked with recruiting some soldiers for a special unit. And lucky you, you've been chosen."

"Thank you?" He couldn't help the querying note, because he wasn't sure why he'd have been chosen. He'd not done anything that made him stand out from anyone else. The first rule a Were learned was never to draw attention.

"You should thank me, because this is an honor, soldier." The colonel had a hard gaze despite his age.

The general grunted. "You're to pack your things and prepare to leave tonight."

"Tonight?" For a second, he forgot to whom he spoke.

The colonel rebuked him. "Is there a problem, Corporal?"

"No, sir. I'll be ready."

Lowin and another guy he'd never seen before—

also a Were; coincidence?—left that night with Colonel Mayflower under the cover of darkness. Lowin and the other fellow eyed each other but said nothing, not with the colonel and driver possibly listening.

They ended up at an airstrip and were flown to a less-active area from the sector where they'd been in defensive posturing for the last few years.

The much smaller military camp boasted few troops, with five Were by his count. Everyone else was human, including the doctor he met the day of his arrival.

"Check in with Dr. Itranj before you join the others," the colonel ordered.

The medical tent proved easy to find with its red cross painted on the canvas door.

As he entered the smell of antiseptic hit him hard. His nose wrinkled.

A man looking through a microscope lifted his head. "Can I help you?" he asked.

"I'm supposed to see a Dr. Itranj."

"Ah, a new recruit. Excellent." The doctor stood, and Lowin took in his appearance. Round face to match a rotund body. Long hair, slicked with grease or sweat, was pulled back from his face. He wore what civilians considered desert wear, meaning beige

slacks, a button-down shirt and a many-pocketed canvas vest. He was missing only the ridiculous hat. Over his outfit, he'd thrown on a stained, long, white coat.

Lowin spent the next hour being examined. He was weighed and measured. His blood pressure was taken, along with vials of blood and swabs from various parts of his body.

"What's all this for?" he asked, surprised by the thoroughness of the exam.

"Needed for the baseline," the doctor muttered. He waved his hand as he went back to his microscope. "You can leave now. I'll call for you when I'm ready."

Ready for what? he wondered.

After exiting, he found there weren't many options for what he should do next. Midafternoon meant no food in the cafeteria tent. He doubted the colonel would want to see him. Munitions were usually off-limits unless he was getting outfitted for an exercise. That left the oversized barracks tent.

Walking in, he paused, quickly realizing every single person inside was Were.

Every.

Single.

One.

Fuck.

Some wore grim expressions. A few were despairing.

He glanced over his shoulder before stepping deeper inside and saying, "Hey."

A man he later came to know as Jarrod grimaced. "I'd say welcome, but that would be a lie."

"What's going on?" he asked.

Jarrod's lips twisted as he said, "Your worst nightmare."

And that was all he'd say. None of them spoke much, mostly because the repercussions could hurt. Sergeant McLean, the same Were who'd selected Lowin, made sure of that. It took several days before he found out the extent of the depravity at the special camp.

A few days after his arrival, Dr. Itranj summoned him to the med tent, and he went, assuming another checkup. He thought nothing of being told to lie on a gurney. But he did protest when the first strap went on his wrist.

"What are you doing?" He tugged and reached to untie it.

"Do not remove it. It's for your own safety."

He highly doubted that as he sought to undo the metal tongue. "I don't need any treatment, I'm fine."

"As a soldier, you signed an agreement that allows

the military to treat you in whatever fashion we deem necessary," Itranj declared.

"So what kind of treatment we talking about?" he asked suspiciously.

"Just an injection. Perfectly safe. Everyone in your unit has already gotten it."

"Does it cause a serious case of the grumps?" Because every single one of his fellow Were at this camp seemed to be sucking on a permanent lemon and one step away from putting a muzzle in his mouth.

"It's to protect you on missions."

"If it's good for me, then why the straps?"

"Because, in rare cases, it can cause involuntary muscle spasms. This is to ensure you don't harm yourself or others."

It sounded plausible, and at that age, he'd remained extremely gullible. He lay like a lamb, rather than a wolf, as Dr. Itranj tethered his wrists and ankles. He even parted his lips for the mouth guard so he wouldn't bite his tongue. Probably not needed. He'd always had a high tolerance for pain.

The needle appeared, full of a murky liquid and bigger than anything he'd ever seen. The doctor swabbed his arm and then poked his flesh. At first, he felt nothing.

Then his arm ignited!

Not literally, and yet, it felt as if it were on fire. He arched, and even through the mouth guard, he uttered a scream as he strained and bucked against the restraints.

Parts of him shifted without volition. His teeth pushed and projected past his lips. His legs twisted into haunches, and fur appeared on parts of his body.

Through it all, the doctor watched, a nurse with a camera recorded, and no one gave a damn that he was in agony. These people didn't give a fuck because, he later found out, they didn't consider him a person. In their purview, they experimented on an animal.

It took hours for the pain and effects of the serum to fade. By the time they dumped him back in the barracks, he was limp, his voice hoarse.

The other Were remained silent as they helped him to bed. The next day, he couldn't get up despite all the sergeant's yelling. Parts of him remained shifted.

It took three days for him to return to normal. The next four, he trained with the others, already just as silent. Because he saw what happened to the animals who stepped out of line.

They went to see the doctor.

Even behaving didn't save him from another visit,

which was why a few weeks after his arrival, he muttered, "We should leave."

Antoine heard him and uttered a short laugh. "It's suicide to try."

"If we escape, they can't hurt us."

"We can't escape, though. Not with the chips." Jarrod slapped his chest.

"What chip?" he stupidly asked.

As if a cruel god listened, he discovered one of the purposes of the chip that same day.

It happened during their exercise period. The colonel paid one of his rare appearances, retaining the familiar smug smirk Lowin had come to know. Fucker thought he was so big and mighty. It got to Pedro. He suddenly screamed, "Filthy human."

Wild-eyed and flushed, Pedro grabbed the colonel by the lapels and lifted him before tossing him across the training field. The colonel hit hard, and Pedro pounced to finish him off. But he twitched in midleap and hit the ground, trembling and quivering, his face a rictus of pain. It lasted—forever—a few minutes. Pedro began to foam at the mouth, and his eyes rolled back. The twitching suddenly stopped.

"Is he dead?" Lowin whispered.

"Nah. But he'll wish they'd killed him," was Jarrod's somber pronouncement.

When Pedro returned several days later, they'd beaten the cocky out of him and subjected him to something that had kept his ears furry. Inhuman. They'd made it impossible for Pedro to escape.

It proved sobering. Lowin kept his nose clean. He submitted to their tests. He went on their missions. Got shot more times than he thought a man could survive.

It was as they dug three bullets out of him that he saw her standing by the edge of his gurney.

"Luna?" He frowned as he said it, recognizing her but confused at the same time. This wasn't right. She shouldn't be here. She was part of his future. Not his past.

Yet, there she stood, eyeing those working on him, her lips pressed into a thin line, unnoticed by the staff as they stitched him up yet again.

When they'd left him with tubes in his arms and the machines around him beeping with familiarity, she finally spoke.

"How long did they torture you?"

Despite it being a dream, he replied, "I was in their control for eleven years."

She sucked in a breath.

"I was their longest-lasting subject." He offered a wry grin.

"*I'm sorry.*"

"*Don't be. I survived.*" But at times, he wished he hadn't.

"*You might have survived, but you haven't forgotten.*"

"*I can't.*" He owed it to those who hadn't escaped with him.

"*I went through something similar. For about the same length of time.*"

"*You were injected and tortured by humans for the sake of science?*" he asked sarcastically.

She nodded.

He stared. "*Wait, you're serious?*"

"*In my case, they took me from an orphanage.*"

"*How old were you?*"

"*Old enough to understand there are very bad people in the world.*"

Beep. Beep. The machinery in his dream room kept going, as if trying to remind him of the ugly. He chose to stare at the pretty woman who might actually understand the darkness inside him.

"*I always knew there were bad folks. I enlisted to get away from them. Turns out they're everywhere. Some just wear more supposedly respectable faces.*"

"*How did you get out?*" she asked.

"*Literally by accident. A chopper went down, and*

the injury I sustained exposed the tracker. I saw my chance and took it."

"To stay hidden, you took your friend's name."

"It seemed safer. See, when I escaped, I didn't know where to go or who to ask for help. I spent some time on the streets, living like an animal. Which, for some reason, reminded me of Lochlan. He proved easy to find, given he did take over the farm after his father died."

"How did you get him to agree to give up his name?"

"I didn't. By the time I found him, he was sick. Real sick. Some sort of malaise the doctors couldn't figure out. But he still wanted to help me. It was him who told me to take over his life, since he didn't have much time left."

"Why didn't you contact the Lykosium?"

His lips twisted. "Because I didn't trust them. I might have been kept in the dark about a bunch of shit, but I was in Hell for eleven years. You hear things during that time. See stuff. It's my belief the Lykosium knew what the military was doing."

"We would never condone experiments."

"But I'll bet your traitor would."

Her lips flattened. "We will find them. I promise you that."

"Going to seal it with a kiss?"

"Flirting again?" She arched a brow.

"Should I have started by saying you're pretty instead?"

Her lips quirked. "When you say it like that..."

"Come here."

"Or what?" she teased. But she leaned over the dream bed.

"I'm injured. Shouldn't you be offering to kiss me better?"

"Can't heal a memory."

"But you could make a nightmare less horrible." He didn't believe for one moment that Luna was truly in his dream. And yet, she acted exactly as he'd expect.

Except for the part where her lips touched his.

Startled, he stopped breathing and froze. Her mouth slanted over his, teasing and caressing. She really did kiss him. And he didn't care if he imagined it. He embraced her right back and might have done more if the machines hooked to him hadn't started beeping, louder and louder and—

ELEVEN

THE INSISTENT CHIMING WOKE LUNA, AND IT took her a second to realize she lay on the bed with Lochlan, her hand flat on his chest, which vibrated with the steady beat of his heart. The dinging of a phone jarred the intimate moment again.

Lochlan abruptly sat up and reached for the nightstand with a muttered, "Shit."

"What's wrong?"

"Something set off the camera."

She eyed him via the light cast by his phone screen, intense and serious. "Are you okay?"

"Why wouldn't I be okay? I have woken up beside a woman before. And while I'd like to say I never fell asleep on a guarding shift, that would be a lie. Sorry. Guess I was more tired than I thought."

He swiped through images on his phone. "False alarm. Looks like people getting into their rooms late." He set the phone aside.

"You were caught in a nightmare. That's what I meant when I asked if you're okay."

"People have bad dreams. It's not a big deal."

"It is when you're reliving your worst moments."

He halted and eyed her. "Excuse me? How would you know what I dreamed?"

"Because I saw it. The way you were recruited. The things they did to you."

His eyes widened. "Wait, you really were inside my head?" His brows quickly drew together. "I never said you could do that."

"It wasn't intentional, I assure you. I simply meant to wake you from your nightmare and somehow got drawn in. Everything I saw..." She trailed off.

"Yeah. It all happened." He paused before adding softly, "What about you? You said you'd also been experimented on."

She nodded. "A single doctor, not related to the military. And instead of faking my death to escape, I was rescued by the Lykosium." She left out the part where there had been no one left to rescue her from by the time the enforcers arrived. The monster had gotten to them all.

"A Lykosium rescue explains your loyalty to them. But forgive me if I don't feel warm and fuzzy in return."

"I'm sure if they—"

"They knew. The things I overheard indicated the Lykosium were in cahoots with those torturing me and the others."

"I refuse to believe that. I'd wager my life this was all the work of the traitor."

"Indicating he's been around for at least two decades, then."

Her mouth opened and shut as the truth smacked her with its obviousness. "I never even thought of that. If he's been covering up for that length of time, then that really narrows the pool of suspects."

"Aren't council positions for life?"

"More or less. A person can retire if they choose, and if someone becomes mentally incapable, they can also be deposed. Then there's attrition by death."

"Whatever. How many council members have been around long enough to have covered up crimes spanning two decades?"

The question knitted her brow, and she gnawed her lower lip. "Five. I think. Maybe six."

"Which narrows the scope of our search."

"Two for sure would never do such a thing," she quickly added. Keira and Lomar were loath to even squish a bug. She couldn't see them condoning the slaughter and torture of their kind.

"Never say never. It's always the nice guy, the perfect neighbor, who ends up being the serial killer." A sobering reminder.

Ding. Ding.

He sighed as his phone started going off again. "Fucking bars close, and it's like Grand Central—" He ceased speaking, and she noticed him frowning before he barked, "Get dressed and ready to go."

"Why?"

"We're about to have company." He tossed the phone on the bed, and she leaned over for a peek at the screen as he rose. She saw someone in combat gear with a gun heading for the stairs.

The sight had her moving quickly, sliding on her shoes, stuffing her wallet and money into her pockets. She eschewed a bra and instead grabbed her jacket.

Lochlan had his ear pressed to the door leading to the balcony. He didn't speak but flashed four fingers at her. Four armed people were heading for their room.

He'd been right to show such caution. She tapped him and canted her head, asking, *Now what?*

They couldn't go out the door. His phone pinged again, and he hissed as he dove for it, turning it to silent. Had anyone heard?

He flipped through images and pointed to the bathroom and mouthed, "No exit." The back of the motel was being guarded.

It appeared as if they'd have to fight. Two against who knew how many. Not great odds.

Let me out, and I'll handle it, she thought. The monster within pulsed, clamoring for blood.

She wouldn't give in. Not now. Not ever.

Lochlan angled his head and looked up. The ceiling of the room was stucco, except for a spot where an oversized access panel had been installed. It was bolted shut. As if that would stop a determined man.

Apparently, he'd planned for this contingency, because he pulled a crowbar from a shopping bag. He placed it in the crevice between the panel and the ceiling. She wondered why he waited.

Bang. Bang. Bang. The shock of the pounding at the door next door drew her gaze. It wouldn't be long before those invading room fourteen realized they'd been fooled. And if they were shifters, they'd smell where she and Lochlan were.

She turned around to see Lochlan had used the noise to cover the sound of him prying the panel open. He cupped his hands, and she didn't hesitate. As she stepped into his laced fingers, he vaulted her into the attic.

Less attic, more a hunched space. She couldn't stand upright, and breathing deeply proved unpleasant because of the smells that came from a space full of mildewy insulation and the scat from mice.

She moved out of the way as Lochlan quickly followed, still silent. How well could those in the next room hear? No idea, and she didn't plan to find out. Lochlan moved past her, partially folded over and moving lightly, keeping his feet firmly planted on the two-by-fours forming a lattice that held up the ceilings of the rooms below them.

She wasn't sure how this would help them until he signaled for her to halt at the far end. He braced himself and gave one solid kick to a trapdoor that dropped into a utility room. He leaped down first and then held out his arms for her. Not that she needed his help. She hesitated, though, as she heard distant shouting.

She leaped down and mouthed, "They're coming."

Lucky for them, the door handle turned from the inside, a safety mechanism to ensure workers didn't get locked in the utility closet. They emerged on the landing at the far end of the motel, right by a set of stairs. A glance back showed someone emerging from room thirteen, spotting them, and yelling, "They're outside!"

"Let's go." Lochlan raced down the steps with her hurrying after him. Those above sprinted to catch them, but their antics drew the attention of other motel guests.

A belligerent male shouted, "What the fuck is going on?"

It delayed their pursuers, but for how long? Luna didn't know how they'd outrun them, especially when Lochlan showed no interest in running toward their vehicle.

He did not appear to have a destination in mind. He ran without looking to see if she followed. Arrogant of him, but at the same time, where else would she go? She'd honestly thought him paranoid. How could they have been found? They'd left no trail.

Perhaps Gerard and his men had come across her SUV in the woods outside the cabin and phoned the information in to the traitor. A shitty theory, because even with her plate number, short of being stopped by a police officer, it wouldn't have been easy to locate.

The shouts behind them dwindled as they turned a corner then another. She would have wondered how far he expected them to bolt, only Lochlan stopped suddenly and dropped down to grab hold of a sewer grate.

"Don't bother. It will be bolted—"

The heavy metal barrier came off to reveal a gaping hole in the ground. "Always have a backup plan," was his reply as he inclined his head. "After you."

A part of her didn't want to go down into that smelly pit.

But she also wanted to live.

She descended into darkness.

TWELVE

LOCHLAN CAREFULLY TUGGED THE GRATE BACK over the hole even as he knew it wouldn't stop anyone from tracking them. Until they camouflaged their scent, it would always give them away. He doubted Luna would like the next part of his plan, because it would involve them getting filthy.

"Now?" she whispered, her eyes glowing in the gloom. A gloom his eyesight had no problem penetrating, one of the tolerable side effects from the experiments.

"Follow me." He didn't actually have a clue where to go, more a general knowledge of sewer systems. They all had to flow somewhere, and best of all, being deep underground and made of concrete made them impenetrable to signals. Because, despite what Luna claimed, he now had no doubt she bore a chip.

To her credit, she didn't complain as they slogged through the muck, mostly rainwater rather than the type that got flushed down toilets. He ensured they walked in the watery sludge, which would hide their tracks, twisting and turning enough that even he couldn't have found his way back.

They didn't hear any signs of pursuit. Glances back didn't show any lights, though they weren't using anything to illuminate their path either. Rather than complain about the dark, Luna followed, one hand on his shoulder to guide her.

The silence pressed thickly on them, which made her voice all the more jarring when she said, "You were right about them tracking me."

He almost fell over in shock. "Should I mark that admission on a calendar?" he quipped, because he doubted she did that often.

"I know when I'm wrong. And in this case, it's a good thing you were around."

"Not going to call me paranoid anymore?"

"Oh, I'll still call you paranoid." She uttered a low laugh. "But rather than argue, I will listen to your advice from now on."

"Less advice and more years of learning how to

live off the radar unnoticed."

"The Feral Pack ranch wasn't well guarded," she remarked.

"Because, for a long time, it wasn't needed. The ranch was a safe place for those looking to lie low."

"Not anymore. Now that it has Pack status, it's not a secret anymore."

"Yeah. Given our newfound fame, I was debating whether to stay or not when shit hit the fan."

"Knowing the traitor gave out information on the smaller packs, leading to their eradication, I guess saying you're safe would be a lie. Everyone is at risk until we find and eliminate him." A low promise.

Rather than dwell on mistakes and lies and traitors, he said, "When you shift, are you always in that hybrid shape?"

She snorted. "That's not a hybrid, and you know it. I'm a monster."

"I wouldn't go so far as to say that. More like a throwback to a more prehistoric version of ourselves."

"Are you calling me a cavewolf?" An incredulous note ended her query.

"Well, you do have the saber teeth."

"Don't remind me," she muttered.

"How many people know about your modified wolf?"

"No one."

"What? Impossible. You were an enforcer. You said yourself that the Lykosium saved you. Someone has to know."

Since she stood behind him, he heard rather than saw her shaking her head. "They rescued me and destroyed the lab with all the notes the doctor kept. Given I feared they'd kill me, I never shifted. They assumed the experiments and trauma left me unable."

"Wait a second. Are you saying you hadn't shifted since your time in that place?"

"Oh, I did, alone, where no one could see. I found places where I could lock myself away to see what would happen. I kept hoping each time that what the doctor did to me would wear off."

"I take it the change is permanent."

"Yes. So I stopped trying and locked away my monster."

"Until Gerard forced it out."

"I didn't even know that was possible."

"It is. It happened to me and the others a few times. Part of their experiments. The difference being we were always fully aware of everything we did. Yet, you don't recall a thing from the moment you shifted to when you woke up in the car. Which is odd, given you spoke to me a few times before that and seemed to understand the situation."

"Not so strange. The experiments did something to me and my wolf. It's as if my beast became its own person. A violent and bloodthirsty thing. Given I couldn't control it, it was just better to never let it out."

"I can't even imagine." A Were usually needed time in the fur. Lochlan got irritable if he couldn't go on four legs every so often.

"I'm used to it."

He almost asked if she missed it, only to realize she probably had no recollection of a time when it didn't cause her stress and pain. Since she was taken at a young age, the trauma would go deep. And yet, look at her. She'd turned her ordeal into a strength and strived to do positive things for Werekind.

Since he couldn't exactly admit his admiration, he changed the subject. "So, where do you think they implanted the tracker?"

"How can we be sure it's me they're tracking and not you?"

"Ain't me they were coming after." He whirled to face her in the dark, seeing the outline of her body.

"We don't know that for sure."

"Are you really going to run with that argument?" he asked, a tad incredulously. "Have you forgotten the fact they were after you in Gerard's forest?"

"According to you."

"Because that's what happened," he snapped. "And there is only one way they could have zeroed in on you so accurately."

"A tracker." A heavy sigh heaved from her. "I hate that you're probably right. It just seems so impossible. Like how could they have done it without me knowing?"

"Easily. Could be you swallowed it in your food."

"Seems unlikely. I could have noticed it, not to mention that would be inefficient, as it would be excreted within days."

"Three to five on average. Seven is usually the safest bet. Unless it gets lodged in the intestine."

She hesitated before saying, "You seem rather knowledgeable about this."

"I was in my early twenties when they recruited me. I lost count of the missions, but some things, the stuff that keeps you alive, or a prisoner, sticks with you forever. Such as how long swallowed items stay inside the body."

"I think we can rule out the edible kind. I've been gone long enough from the Lykosium base of operation that I should be clear."

"Unless someone followed you and got to you when you were unaware. Did you order room service at any time since your departure?"

"A part of me wants to mock your paranoia. And yet, now I can't help but wonder."

"Honestly, I think a chip was most likely embedded in your flesh. And before you claim you'd have noticed, no, you wouldn't. An injection—"

She interrupted. "I think I'd have noticed someone poking me with a needle."

"Unless they drugged you and did it while you slept. And before you argue you'd have felt it the next day, let me say, no, you wouldn't necessarily. They could have placed a tiny one anywhere in your body. It doesn't need to be large to function."

"But it does need some size if they want it to have any kind of range that will get picked up," she countered.

"Correct, meaning if yours is an embedded implant, it must not be where you or others would notice it."

"How deep could it go?" she mused aloud, following as he turned yet another corner. They traversed under a grate, the faint glint from the streetlight above giving her limited visibility.

"I take it you've never had a throbbing pain deep in any part of your body or an unexplained ache that eventually went away or felt an oddity under your skin." He caught the faint shake of her head as he halted at an access tunnel that branched off in four directions.

"Like I said, I'd have noticed."

"Would you? You heal ridiculously fast. Guess that's a good thing since we don't have a sewing kit to stitch you up when that tracker comes out."

"Assuming there is a tracker inside me."

"Are we back to arguing about that again? Let me have a look and we can settle that question once and for all." He placed his knapsack on a pipe running around the open area.

"Is this your way of asking to see my bare ass?"

"Actually, I doubt your ass would have it. Too much chance you'd notice something when you sit. Shoulder blades too. My guess is it would be in a section of your back that can't be easily reached by you, or revealed by a crop top or low-slung pants."

"I'm starting to wonder how many people you've chipped," she quipped, peeling off her jacket and laying it on a dry spot.

Enough to know some of the people deserved to have their every move watched, but he didn't say that aloud. "Let's just leave it at I know what I'm looking for. Pull up your shirt."

"Should I drop my pants too?" she sassed.

"Only if I don't locate anything on your back." He kept his reply professional, because this was serious. They couldn't have their every step dogged by those people with the guns.

"Not sure what you think you'll find in the dark," she grumbled, but she lifted her shirt, revealing the strong, smooth lines of her back, the taper of her waist, and, at this angle, the swell of a breast. She was a well-shaped woman, her body full-figured and toned, and her face showed the character of her years. Just his type.

However, this wasn't the moment to express his admiration. Security came before seduction.

He turned his attention to the indent of her spine. In the gloom, it proved hard to see any kind of shadow under her skin. Even with good light, he might miss the device, which was why he'd have to use his hands.

"I'll have to touch you to locate the chip," he murmured softly. "At times, I'll be pressing firmly to ensure there's nothing there."

"I can't believe you're announcing your intent to grope me," she grumbled.

"If you feel uncomfortable, tell me to stop, and I will."

"I'm not a wilting flower who can't handle being palpated. Just get it over with." Luna held herself rigidly as he palmed her flesh, his spread fingers resting on her shoulder blades. With their constant movements, she might notice if they rubbed over a foreign object under her skin. He slid his hands down below her shoulders, pushing at her toned body, alert for any sign of something unnatural.

Her breath hitched.

"Are you okay?" he asked. "Did you feel something?"

"Your hands are warm." She sounded surprised.

"I always run hot." It had made his time in the arid Middle East difficult. At the ranch, he slept with the windows open and a fan running.

He stroked his hands down her frame and felt her shiver. But not from cold, he suspected.

"Have you ever actually found a tracking device by touch?" she asked, her words higher pitched than usual.

"Yes. Twice." He'd helped men in his squad—

never women, because the military apparently had other uses for female Were, which seemed quite ominous—locate and remove trackers in the hopes they could escape. If they'd gotten away, Lochlan didn't know, because he'd seen none of them again. Could have been because the C Squad had changed locations after every breach. Although, according to the colonel, he'd always found the runaways and eliminated them.

"I'm starting to think maybe I'm the one who isn't paranoid enough," she murmured. "You'd think after what I experienced I'd hold a more suspicious view of the world."

"Maybe it's a good thing you don't. It ain't easy always thinking the worst might happen."

"Did you still feel that way even after you lived at the ranch? From what I saw, you appeared to be living a normal life. No booby traps or cameras. Although I guess it's possible you just hid your surveillance well."

He grunted. "More like I got complacent." His fingers tickling down her back drew more quivers from her, and dammit, he could scent her interest. "And if I'm being honest, I got to the point I kind of didn't give a shit. I spent a good chunk of my life living in Hell then the next part afraid of going back.

It occurred to me it would have been easier to just get it over and done with."

"You think the military would have dragged you back?"

"Or killed me, which was my preference. I would prefer to die than ever go through that again."

"You and me both." She turned, and his fingers slid from her back to her stomach. He froze rather than remove them. Her gaze met his. "You and I have much in common."

He curved his fingers around her waist and drew her close. "Don't play coy. You know it's more than that, what this feeling is."

The mating instinct. A thing he wanted to deny.

"I do." A low admission. "It would never work."

Of course it wouldn't. A man damaged and wanted like him could never have someone like Luna. "I'm sorry. I know it wouldn't. You deserve better than an ornery rogue."

At his claim, laughter burst from her, low and bitter. "Me? It's you who could do better than me."

"Aren't we a pair?" he huffed. "Both convinced we are terrible for each other. Maybe that's what makes it the right fit."

"You don't want to be with me," she said, quite seriously. "I'm unloved for a reason."

The more she spoke, the more he heard himself in her words.

"Maybe it's time that changed," he suggested.

"Maybe, but now is not the time to explore that."

"When?"

"When it's less dangerous. If I can't expose the traitor, then chances are I'll be portrayed as a council member gone rogue, and they'll declare open season on me."

"Surely those who know you wouldn't believe you'd do anything to harm Werekind."

"It doesn't take much to sway the masses. Or have you forgotten all the crises the media have gotten the world to froth over?" As soon as one problem faded, the media whipped people into a frenzy about the next hot topic.

"We won't let it get that far."

"Even if we do stop the traitor, you and I—it can't ever go anywhere."

"Why not?"

She blinked at him, and her voice held a hint of incredulity when she said, "You've seen me. I'm a monster. The doctor made sure I could never be with anyone."

The conviction in her words actually hurt him and only made him feel closer to her, because he well understood the belief he would forever be unworthy. "Perhaps that's why we met, because of all the people in the world, you and I are the only ones who could ever understand each other." The words spilling from his lips shocked him. Blame it on the intimacy of the moment. In the dark, anything could be said.

"Understanding doesn't change the facts." She leaned her face against his chest and huffed a hot breath. "Despite how we feel right now, it won't work. You deserve better."

"Says who?" he argued.

"Says me. I'm broken, Lochlan," she admitted against his chest, and he felt the heat of tears. "It's more than the fact I shift into a monster. I'm too old for children."

"Pretty sure I'm just as old as you, possibly older."

"Even if I weren't, I'm barren, dammit."

"And I'm infertile, so what's your point?"

She stilled. "You have an answer for everything."

"While you have an excuse." He lay his cheek on the top of her head. "The fucked-up part is you sound just like me. Well, me before I met you, and I found a reason to argue. Hard as it is to believe, I think you and I were meant to find each other."

"The idea of accepting you as my mate is terrifying," she whispered, "because what if I hurt you? What if one day you look at me with disgust because I'll never be perfect or whole?" The raw honesty plucked at him.

"And there you go sounding like me again. Which is why, as much as this scares us both, it's worth fighting for. Maybe, finally, we don't have to be alone." Because, even among people, a man was sometimes an island, the waves of others lapping his shores but never staying.

"You make it sound possible."

"Because it is." He wanted to make it happen. With that realization, he drew her upward so that he might press his mouth to hers.

The kiss started out soft. Sweet. A gentle caress of exploration. It devolved into nipping and sucking, the harsh pants of their excitement giving way to passion. His hands dug into her waist, pulling her closer. He was stroking her skin as he kissed her, kneading her flesh, when he felt the hard hint of something that didn't belong.

He paused before whispering, "I found it."

He wished he'd kept quiet a moment longer as she sighed against his lips and said, "Cut it out."

THIRTEEN

Well, that had ended quicker than expected.

Luna vacillated between annoyance that the kiss had come to an abrupt finish and irritation that she'd been chipped and had never once suspected.

"It will hurt," Lochlan warned as he kept palpating the area where he'd found the foreign object.

"Not as much as the traitor will who put it in me," was her solemn promise.

Lochlan tried to be gentle as he used a pocketknife clipped to his knapsack to slice through her skin. They had nothing to freeze the area, and she had only her fist to bite down on. As if she'd scream in pain.

The incision hurt, but she could handle it. Rather than give in to her primal rage, she gnawed on her knuckles.

They marked me.

For how long, she had no idea. One day was too much. How dare they? How dare someone track her movements? Spy on her?

Never mind the fact her job often had her ordering the same for Packs and their members. She'd chipped Kit from a young age out of fear someone would steal him from her because he was different.

To think she, one of the chosen few, had been unwittingly supplying the traitor with information all this time. Rage burned.

The ambush by Gerard? Her fault.

Kit getting kidnapped? Also because of her.

How many other casualties had she inadvertently caused?

It didn't take much cutting and poking before Lochlan softly said, "It's out."

She whirled to see the bloody object in his hand, barely the size of a stamp. Yet, it seemed immense when she considered it had resided in her body, an unwanted visitor.

"Gimme." She held out her hand, and he dropped it into her palm.

For a second, she closed her fist around the tracker, ready to crush it into oblivion. She held back, as it occurred to her the tiny device could be useful. "So I know you're good at evading capture, but let me ask, how are your ambush skills?"

She could barely see his face in the gloom as he replied, "Should I be afraid to ask?"

Luna held up the chip. "This might provide us with an opportunity to get some answers."

"You want to set a trap." He caught on quickly.

"We find a location that is advantageous to us. Then we place the chip there, drawing those tracking me, allowing us to capture at least one who can answer some questions."

"Definitely doable. However, you do realize they won't come quietly? We will have to use force. Possibly even deadly force."

"I'm aware of that and fine with it. After all, those we're dealing with are breaking our laws. And they know the punishment for that."

Death.

"If you're good, then I'm good. It's probably our quickest bet to finding out who's giving them their orders. But until we can lay a proper trap, we need to lie low and keep that thing"—he pointed to the device—"from projecting our location once we get out of this concrete maze."

To conceal the signal required Lochlan to fetch something from the surface.

The twenty minutes he was gone felt like an eternity to Luna, alone in that dark sewer with only her thoughts and seesawing emotions. She replayed their conversation and the kiss.

She wanted him.

She shouldn't.

She did.

But couldn't.

Before she figured out what to do, he returned from an all-night corner store, where he'd bought a metal cannister with a cartoon pig on the front and something about bacon being the fifth food group. He'd also bought three water bottles. They each drank one, but the third was poured into the cannister to submerge the chip. Between the metal and the water, the device signal should be interrupted. In case it wasn't, they'd have to work fast.

As they emerged from the sewer, she took a big cleansing breath. "Where to?" she asked.

"We need a place to plot, preferably with a shower."

"Another motel?" she asked as they headed up the quiet street lined with closed stores.

"Nope." He kept glancing around at the buildings they walked past.

She finally asked, "What are you looking for?"

"Basement apartment."

"Which will likely be occupied," she remarked.

"We'll find one that's not." He abruptly stopped by a window covered with bars. "Here."

The glass pane was open a crack, and fumes from fresh paint wafted out. The window lacked any curtains, but her sight couldn't penetrate farther inside.

"You're sure it's empty?" she asked as he headed down some concrete steps to a door marked B.

"Guess we'll soon find out."

Before she could ask how they'd get in, he gave the door a firm shove. It popped open, and he ushered her inside. A stronger smell of paint hit, and she grimaced. An acute sense of smell could suck at times.

The apartment was indeed empty, if one ignored the tarps on the floor and the boxes of tools. The apartment appeared to be getting more than a fresh coat of paint on the walls. The kitchenette had only half its cupboard doors, while the rest appeared to still be in boxes, waiting for installation. The fridge still had its store tags, and that was where Lochlan headed, pulling off the tape to open the freezer. He stuck the metal bottle inside and shut the appliance. Even more protection against a leaky signal.

There were two doors. One led to an empty bedroom with more drop cloths, and the other led to a bathroom. He shut the bathroom door before turning on the light, forcing her to blink at the sudden brightness.

She almost prayed before turning on the shower taps. Water ran clean and clear, cold, but to her delight, it soon turned warm. From his knapsack, Lochlan produced soap and even a towel.

She arched a brow. "You're very prepared."

"Like you said before, I've done this kind of thing in the past. One of the things I learned was to always have bathing stuff with me in case I had to do dirty things to mask my scent."

"You should go first, since you're so well prepared."

"Or we could save time and shower together," he suggested flatly, and yet, she caught the hint of heat in his words. Logically, they shouldn't both be naked at the same time, because that would leave them vulnerable—but also because it could lead to other things.

However, there might not ever be another time. Another chance. Luna had spent her life serving others. First, the doctor, and then the Lykosium. With the exception of her adoption of Kit, when had she ever truly done something for herself?

"We're wasting hot water," was her reply as she pulled off her shirt and draped it over the sink vanity.

Would he accept the invitation?

FOURTEEN

LOCHLAN HAD BEEN SURE LUNA WOULD LAUGH him off or tell him where to go. He certainly hadn't expected her to strip, her gaze holding invitation and challenge.

Having never been a coward, even when frightened out of his mind, and knowing what sex would mean for them, he followed suit.

She had to know if they did this there would be no turning back. Their kind had a few quirks besides baying at the moon and turning furry. When a pair who were fated to be mates met, there was an awareness, a need, a hunger that, once sealed with intercourse, formed a bond that only death could break.

He could say no. She'd never beg. She'd also never invite him again.

Lochlan stepped into the shower and dragged her against him for a kiss. The hot spray hit them but felt cool compared to the erupting passion. Their mouths clung and caressed, hungry and clumsy as they lost all finesse in their eagerness.

He tried to retain some semblance of control, snaring the soap and doing his best to run it over her flesh. It proved to be almost more than he could handle. He wanted nothing more than a quickie with her back against the wall, but she deserved better than his impatience.

His hand with the bar of soap slid between her thighs, and she moaned into his mouth. He tried to wash her and she him, their hands stroking and soaping. Her hot, slick flesh trembled as he stroked over her. Her short gasps of pleasure drove him wild. His cock bobbed, hard and ready, his hips thrusting as she reached out and grabbed him. Her urgency as she stroked his slick length matched his. If she kept touching him like that, he'd come for sure.

He wasn't ready for that. He broke off the kiss so he could drop to his knees. He wanted to worship at her mound. He pushed his face against the vee of her thighs to part them. She did one better and draped a leg over his shoulder and tugged his hair as he gave her a more intimate kiss. He buried his tongue into her sex, probing and flicking her to tease before working on her sensitive clit, his tongue playing with the engorged nub.

She rode his face, hips pumping, pushing against his mouth. He kept up his tongue work on her clit but brought some fingers into play. He thrust into her, feeling her tighten, her hips still pumping.

He groaned against her, vibrating her flesh, which only served to have her squeezing harder. He finger-fucked her while he licked her button. Flicked it. Tugged it with his lips until she panted harshly and quivered. Her pleasure wetted his tongue, fed his arousal, but the ambrosia came when she orgasmed, hips thrusting one last time as her whole body seized in climax.

She came good. She came hard.

But he wasn't done yet.

Need wanted him to bury his cock to the hilt. But once he did, there would be no turning back.

There was still time for her to say no.

He kissed her and whispered, "Tell me to stop."

"I don't want you to stop," was her reply, without any hesitation.

He was only a man in front of his mate, needing what only she could offer. He palmed her lean ass cheeks and lifted her, aligning her slick core with his cock. A grunt escaped as he fitted the thick head of his shaft between her lips.

She gasped. "Yes. Lochlan."

Her voice had him thrusting deep, pushing into her trembling flesh. Despite her back being against the wall and his hands firmly gripping her ass, her legs wrapped around his flanks to lock him in tight.

As if he'd go anywhere.

A groan. A grunt. Lochlan pistoned into her while her fingers dug into his back, and she panted, "Yes."

His shaft slipped in and out of her, faster and faster, until she came again, a tightening that drew his own orgasm.

"Fuck. Yes." He closed his eyes as the pleasure took him.

The certainty. The inexorableness.

She's mine.

As that thought sank in, they emerged from the shower to plan their ambush.

Because the fight had become personal. *Someone wants to hurt my mate.* And that couldn't be allowed to happen.

Now if only she wouldn't argue when he told her the plan he'd concocted.

FIFTEEN

"YOUR PLAN SUCKS," LUNA DECLARED.

"Like fuck it does." Her naked lover—*oh, say it, her mate*—sat cross-legged on the floor in front of her. They had no lights on and relied on what spilled through the window from the street to illuminate his rudimentary plan, played out by a screwdriver and some balled-up painter's tape.

"It will work. Trust me," he stated.

She stared at his strong jawline, which was covered in a few days' growth. So handsome. *Mine*. Already, she wanted him inside her again.

"What if you're wrong?"

"I won't let you get hurt." An ominous reply that could mean so many things, but judging by the hard glint in his gaze, he'd kill for her.

That led to her pouncing on him for a second round of really good sex. Like, *really* good. Especially once she stopped freaking out about the fact that their involvement changed everything.

Maybe it was time she stopped thinking she didn't deserve love. Maybe it was time for both of them to heal. Together.

Eventually, not wanting to get caught, they had to leave their hiding spot. Being on foot made it easy to stop at a food shop just opening for breakfast. A hot croissant fresh from the oven was heaven but not as delicious as the whipped foam she sucked off his upper lip.

They walked for the better part of that morning before finding the perfect place to plant the tracking chip, a busy family diner with a constant flow of patrons.

Luna waited out of sight while Lochlan went inside to plant it. He returned with that loose-hipped, long-legged strut that tightened everything inside her.

A man shouldn't be so sexy. How could she think she deserved him?

He smiled.

At her.

And her alone.

She needed to stop questioning it and enjoy the gift she'd been given. Especially since it could be taken from her at any moment.

As they hightailed it out of the parking lot, he gripped her hand and tugged her across the busy street to an apartment building. It wasn't hard to get in. He had her pause by the front door for a kiss, and when someone unlocked the door to enter, he grabbed the door and muttered, "Thanks, man, got a little distracted."

"Sure, no problem," was the reply as the male resident moved to the mailboxes to get his mail. They got on the elevator, the kind that required a card to move between floors. When the doors shut, she whispered, "Now what?"

"You kiss me again."

He didn't just kiss her—he ignited her from head to toe. He had her lifted and grinding against him when the elevator doors opened, and a man cleared his throat.

Lips soft with passion, Lochlan eyed the resident holding his stash of mail. "Nine, please, before I forget again." He turned a half-lidded gaze on her and purred, "Blame my vixen."

She shivered and dragged him closer for another

smooch. The passenger on the elevator with them sighed but keyed in their floor.

The guy got out on four, but Luna didn't pull herself from Lochlan's embrace until the doors opened again on the ninth floor.

"I think we've arrived," she said.

"Not yet, but you will. Soon." He held her hand as he led her down the hall to the stairwell. But rather than go down, he encouraged her to go up one more floor, following signs that said Rooftop Terrace.

They had no sooner spilled onto the open area atop the apartment building than Lochlan scanned the space, looking for the presence of anyone else.

This time of day in midweek, and with a sharp bite in the cool air, no one partook of the almost park-like space. The door slammed shut, and a second later, her back was pressed into it as Lochlan resumed the kiss from the elevator.

His hand ended up inside her pants, and she almost bit his tongue as he made her come from fingering her.

Her breathing hitched as she said, "Your turn."

Rather than keep blocking the doorway in case someone tried to exit, they dragged chairs to the glass railing that offered a perfect view of the parking lot and streets around the diner where he'd planted the

tracking chip. As they took up their watching posi-
tion, backs to the door onto the terrace, she returned
the favor and tugged his cock until his hips twitched.
Pity she wore pants. A skirt would have let her
discreetly straddle him and have her fun.

Maybe next time, she'd be better prepared. The
fact she'd assumed a future with him shocked her.

"What's wrong, sweetheart? You look like you
saw a ghost," Lochan murmured as he tucked himself
away. "Was my come face that terrifying?"

The statement caught her off guard, and she
laughed. "I can't believe you said that."

"And you haven't replied yet if it was scary."

"Your face is fine." She blushed as she recalled
just how she'd made him look—intense and focused
on her. "Just wishing I'd worn something with easier
access."

He laced his fingers with hers. "Next time."

More might have been said, or done, except a
woman carrying a knitting basket joined them on the
terrace. She sat on the far side but in sight.

No matter. Luna leaned against him, and from
their place of prominence, they watched the diner
and parking lot, waiting to see when the bait was
taken. Unlike her, he wanted to observe those
hunting rather than lure them somewhere remote

and take them out, one by one. Back at the apartment they'd squatted in, Lochlan had quickly shot down Luna's idea.

"Even if we're sly," he'd said, *"if the traitor sends more people than expected, we'll never manage to take them all out. Not only do we have to worry they might be shooting to kill, there's also a massive potential for capture."*

"Then what do you suggest?"

"Patience. We watch them and wait for the right time where we can act and not alarm civilians." Another word for humans.

"What if they're too careful and we never get a chance at them?" she'd argued.

"They can't be cautious forever, and we only need one."

Capture the one in charge, and they'd get their answers. But how would they identify that person?

Lochlan had had a dour prediction for that part. *"I'm going to wager it's someone you've seen before. Maybe a former enforcer. Could even be a current Lykosium employee high up in the food chain."*

She didn't want to believe him. She'd always been all about protecting, and those around her had seemed to share that passion. But one of them—possibly more than one—was a liar.

And if Gerard could be believed, the traitor was Kit's father.

The busy restaurant where they'd planted the chip made a terrible place for the Lykosium agents to converge. If they wore uniforms, they'd stick out and draw too much notice. Lochlan banked on the theory they would wait for Luna to emerge from the diner so they could ambush her in a more discreet place.

Luna and Lochlan watched from the nearby rooftop, and within the hour, she spotted an over-sized SUV with blacked-out windows, hardly incon-spicuous, that parked at the back of the restaurant parking lot.

"Looks like they took the bait," Lochlan murmured.

"Let's go get them." Luna started to rise, but he tightened his grip on her hand.

"Not yet. The trap isn't fully sprung."

"You're waiting for them to get out of the vehi-cle? I don't think they're planning to anytime soon."

"Because the place is hopping. They're not stupid. They know they can't do anything in a diner full of people."

"How long are they going to sit there, though, before one of them goes inside and figures out I'm not in there?"

"I don't think we'll have to wait too long."

"You sound rather sure of that."

"It's called confidence, sweetheart."

"Is that another word for 'arrogant'?"

"Not arrogant if I'm right."

"Let's say someone goes inside. How does that help us? We're up here. They're down there. By the time we get to their level—"

"They'll be gone. Yup. On a wild-goose chase."

She blinked at him. "I think you're going to have to explain the plan again, because I'm not grasping it. I thought we were supposed to lure them and then follow so we could split one off from the rest to question."

"That is exactly the plan. With one minor adjustment, we're going to send the muscle after a decoy while we talk to the brains of the operation."

Hold on a second... "You didn't just drop the chip inside, did you?" she accused.

"In order for the tracker's movements to appear natural to those watching, it requires motion. So I removed it from the cannister and gave it to someone."

"Who?" she said, almost squeaking.

"That woman." He pointed to a tiny person in the distance who sported a similar build to Luna, though her hair was less silvery and more blond. Lochlan explained, "Our decoy was sitting down to lunch when I bumped into her table and dropped the chip in her purse."

"She'll get hurt."

"Only if they're stupid. They're not going to approach her in public. They'll shadow her steps, and when they swoop in to abduct her, her scent will reveal the ruse."

"That only takes care of the group in the SUV. Who does that leave for us to ask questions?"

Lochlan pointed to a car across the lot from the SUV, a tinted-windowed BMW. "I'm going to wager that luxury rental holds their boss."

A frown creased Luna's brow. "Seems a little conspicuous."

"So conspicuous you haven't paid it any attention at all."

She bit her lower lip. "Point taken. I saw it and thought it was driven by either the owner of the place or a suit having lunch with his mistress."

"How sexist of you."

"You have to admit it's a pretentious car."

"Maybe they love it for its heated seats."

"Heated seats are overrated."

"What do you like to drive?" he asked as the

decoy Luna drove her car out of the parking lot, the SUV right behind.

"I don't often drive." Her lips turned down. "My duties keep me in the office more often than I like."

"Maybe it's time you told your duties to relax so you can get out more. Ever ridden an ATV?" A casual question.

She shook her head.

"When this is over, I want to take you on a trail I know."

Her lips curved. "I'd like that." Mostly because he wanted to spend time with her.

Gawds. She was turning into a sap already. The mating appeared to have softened her. Taken her edge.

As he drew Luna to her feet, he kissed her.

"Ready?" he whispered against her mouth.

With him? She was ready for anything.

SIXTEEN

LOCHLAN HATED THE NEXT PART OF THE PLAN, even as he'd suggested it. It had occurred to him that whoever was overseeing the operation to extract Luna would probably be watching from afar.

If he was right, and the BMW held that person, then the best way to distract them? Send their target straight for them.

Luna sauntered up to the BMW's driver side door and rapped on the window.

Lochlan really hoped no one shot at her, because at such close range, even super healing might not be enough.

The window rolled down, and the smarmy fellow inside opened his mouth to say, "Well, if it isn't—eep."

The abrupt halt occurred when Luna grabbed the man by the shirt and yanked him through the window.

She was stronger than she should be. He'd felt that strength earlier. Her passion, unbridled, had been a thing to see. Powerful and beautiful.

Luna dragged the driver to his feet and off them as she lifted him off the ground. Hopefully, nobody watched and wondered about an overly strong woman assaulting a man from a BMW.

Lochlan moved closer. "Do you recognize him?"

She cocked her head. "No." She gave the man she held a shake. "Who sent you?" Her eyes swirled with all the colors of the rainbow, and her nostrils flared as she inhaled.

And got nothing, Lochlan would wager. The man had been doused in a scent remover. If he couldn't see him, Lochlan wouldn't have known the fucker was there.

"Let me go," the man demanded.

"I will when you tell me who sent you." Luna didn't budge.

The idiot blurted out, "I don't know what you're talking about." A lie.

"Are you refusing to answer?" Her voice lowered to a growl.

The man turned his eyes on Lochan. "Call her off. I ain't done nothing."

"You presume to think I have that kind of control over her."

"He doesn't, in case you were wondering," Luna confided.

The man's gaze darted back to Luna. "You wouldn't dare hurt me in public."

"It's the only reason you're not bleeding yet. So what do you say we go somewhere private?" Luna cooing sweetly was the most terrifying thing.

The man blanched. "My crew—"

She arched a brow. "Ah, so you're not here alone."

The reminder that he had a team bolstered the scentless idiot. "I've got people with me. Enough to take care of both of you."

"Pity they're long gone, following a false trail that's far enough away now that they can't help you." Lochlan shut down all hope. Sometimes despair could be helpful in convincing someone to spill their guts. If not, then the painful bits started.

The man held firm. "You can't hurt me. If you do, it will be twice as bad for her. She's a wanted criminal."

"By whose order?" she asked. "Who sent you? Who is the traitor on the council? Tell me."

The man's eyes widened. "No. No. No! I said nothing. Turn it off—"

His scream ended when his head exploded.

SEVENTEEN

THEIR ONLY LEAD, A MAN WHO'D NOT SHARED HIS
name, died messily. Abruptly. Remotely. As in,
someone sent a wireless command and *kaboom*.

Brains everywhere. It would have been laughable
if it weren't so frustrating.

One thing did become crystal clear. The traitor
would stop at nothing to keep his secret. Even kill his
own allies.

Since they couldn't exactly walk around with
fleshy bits and blood on their faces, they stole the
BMW and abandoned what was left of the body
behind. Hopefully, nobody had gotten any video.
Especially of her assaulting the guy. A guy who'd
gone *splat*.

Gulp.

Luna didn't feel sick because of what had happened but because the monster within her found it thrilling.

Killing should never be considered fun. Although she wouldn't deny she'd felt satisfaction when she'd taken out every single person who'd had a hand in placing her with the doctor. Especially Sister Francine. *May she rot in Hell.*

"We need to clean up." They'd driven about twenty minutes, enough to get out of the main part of town, before he pulled the BMW over.

"Don't you mean wipe off the brains?" was her almost-hysterical riposte. "This is crazy. How can I fight that kind of evil? Why bother?"

"You bother because of the Kits in this world. And the Poppys and every other Were who deserves saving. Because you're strong and good."

She snorted. "You wouldn't say that if you'd seen what I've done."

"Sometimes being good requires you to do ugly things."

Her head dropped forward. "But I'm so tired of fighting."

"Would it help if I said you're not alone?" He tilted her chin up.

"Why would you want to get involved? You saw

what just happened. The traitor blew up someone's head!"

"Yeah, let's avoid that, if you don't mind."

With a sob, she threw herself at him, for the first time dropping the pretense of being brave. "I don't want you to die."

"I don't want me to die either. And I especially don't want to see you hurt. Which is why we are going after this fucker and taking him out."

"You think we can?" She held his hands and looked him in the face.

His crooked grin reassured her almost as much as his words. "Together, we can do anything."

Including booking a hotel online using a prepaid credit card he'd purchased earlier. The location they selected provided an electronic key that meant no checking in at a front desk. They used an app on his smartphone to beep open the door for the rear parking lot, and then they went straight up the stairs to their room on the second floor.

They showered together, soaping and rinsing twice. Then he scrubbed the tub, serious about his task, while she bagged the bloody clothes. There was no time to indulge in the passion that simmered between them with every look and touch. Not yet. They still had to make themselves safe.

They didn't stay at that hotel but moved again, leaving the BMW behind, the dirty clothes stashed inside to be destroyed by fire. The lighter fluid he'd poured over the front seats ignited the moment the lit packet of matches hit it. Hand in hand, they walked a few blocks to reach a seedy motel that preferred no names and cash.

Only once Lochlan had secured the room did they make love by the neon light filtering through the curtains. Their soft, sensual coming together of bodies led to spooning afterward, followed by hard and furious, pounding sex that left red furrows on his back and a satisfied smile on his face.

She probably wore the same look. What she wouldn't give for more alone time with him before having to deal with the traitor she'd have to confront.

Which led to her having an idea.

Lochlan proved skeptical.

"Let me get this straight. You want us to live in a shipping container for a week—"

"About ten days, actually."

He blinked at her. For a man, he had insanely thick lashes. "Are you insane?"

"It's the most discreet way of getting to Europe without any trails." The current council's seat of power was in Bulgaria.

He raked a hand through his hair. "You want to spend ten days in a coffin."

"I promise you'll be able to walk around inside it. Think of it as a tiny home for not even two weeks."

"You know I live on a huge ranch, right?"

She clasped his hands. "Trust me."

He did. They ended up in an eight-by-about-fourteen-foot shipping container with a bucket to shit and piss in, a crate of nonperishable food to eat, and an air mattress with a few blankets.

With nothing else to do, they fucked.

They talked. About everything. Even their time as prisoners.

They fucked some more.

They slept by day and haunted the ship at night, because Lochlan refused to stay cooped up for the entire trip. Luna might have argued against that, until he let her know she could use an actual bathroom at night.

"A real toilet and shower?" she'd said with such *excitement.*

He stood guard while she did her thing. To keep in shape, Lochlan went for a jog each night, and she kept watch, ululating if a crew member went wandering. By the third night, rumors of an evil spirit on board kept most sailors in their berths at night.

Alas, as with all cruises, this one came to an end, and Lochlan had to admit he'd had a great time. Once the ship docked in France, and before Customs agents could board, he and Luna fled the ship.

They'd made it to Europe. Now for the next leg of their trip.

Destination: the Lykosium castle. The seat of Were power.

EIGHTEEN

THAT NIGHT, WRAPPED IN LOCHLAN'S ARMS somewhere in France, Luna dreamed...

The trip that took Luna away from the orphanage filled her with hope. The most she'd felt since the night she lost Mama. The doctor seemed friendly, sitting with her in the back seat of the large car. He had so many questions, most of them easy to answer— name, age, favorite color, favorite food.

He also had other queries—home address, parents' full names, names of aunts, uncles, grandparents. He frowned slightly when she claimed to have no relatives.

"Surely you have a home."

"Mama and I used to live in a blue car, but then it stopped working, and a man with a big belly came

*and said we had to move it, only Mama couldn't, so
she only let me pack my favorite outfit and Floofloo."*
*The stuffed toy that she'd lost that night in the woods
along with everything else.*

"Unusual. What of your Pack?"

She frowned as she repeated, "My what?"

*"Did you ever live with others like you? People
who could change into wolves?"*

Her lips clamped tight.

*"Don't be shy. I know all about your special abil-
ity. You can talk about it with me."*

"Mama said to keep it a secret."

*"Your mama was right. But unfortunately, she's
gone, which means you need someone you can talk to
and trust."*

*It would be so nice to not be alone. Starved for
affection, Luna talked and talked. The entire two days
they drove, she told the doctor everything he wanted to
know. And in return, he showed her kindness, fed her
exactly what she wanted, even though the waitress
eyed Luna askance as she asked for extra sausage and
bacon and ham with her breakfast.*

*When the car, with its silent driver, finally pulled
to a stop in front of a grand house, Luna bubbled with
excitement. "Is this where you live?"*

"Yes, and now you do too."

The room assigned to her was beautiful. Large, with walls papered in silver and pink. The wooden floors were polished to gleaming. The windows, almost floor-to-ceiling, were covered in filmy curtains that nearly hid the bars that covered them. It occurred to her as she stepped into the room, which smelled strongly of ammonia and other cleaners, that the thick door locked from the outside.

For furniture, she had very little. A large mattress lay directly on the floor, but it was the sight of a bolted metal ring on the floor next to it that froze Luna. The wood around it had been cleaned so much that it was a lighter color. It had been scrubbed down to the bare surface, and yet, even that couldn't erase the taint of blood.

Danger!

Luna whirled to run, but the doctor grabbed her in a firm grip that had her snapping and snarling, "Let me go."

"You need to calm down."

"I don't want to live here."

"Too late."

"No." *She huffed, pulling against his grip to no avail.*

"And to think we'd been getting along so famously," *the doctor chided as he tsked and shook his head.*

"*You said I could trust you.*" Betrayal threatened to swamp her with despair.

"*You still can. But at the same time, I understand what you are. A werewolf. A dangerous monster if left unchecked.*"

"*I'm not,*" she protested.

"*I don't think those at the orphanage would agree.*"

She hung her head. "*I never meant to hurt anyone.*"

"*I know you didn't, which is why I am going to help you.*"

She eyed the ring in the floor. "*Are you going to tie me up?*" She remembered seeing a dog tethered to a similar device, its whole world reduced to a tiny pacing circle.

"*Behave, and I won't have to.*"

By behave, he meant contain the wolf.

She did. Except for on the full moon, when the doctor told her to let it out for observation. It hurt to change. Hurt because she wanted to run and feel the fresh air on her face. Instead, her whole world was a bedroom with a small, attached bathroom. Her windows didn't open, and they teased her with a view of outside. The changing seasons bred a melancholy in her that no amount of reading could distract from.

For years, she did her best to behave, not that it made a difference. *Dr. Adams—such an innocuous name for such an evil man—started out content with observing and asking questions.* How do you feel? Is the beast separate? *The occasional vials of blood he took were easy to tolerate.*

His biggest positive, though, was he brought her books on a variety of subjects. She devoured the knowledge even as she couldn't use it.

Under Adams' watchful eye, she grew, and during every full moon, she shifted, her wolf more and more agitated by the confined space.

Sometime in her early teens, after weeks of loud thumping in the room next to hers, the doctor unveiled a surprise. She now had access to a gym, replete with mats and bolted bars for exercise. That didn't completely quell the building energy within, though.

As she got older, the doctor's tone shifted. No longer content to merely study, he began experimenting on her, first by feeding her things that were poisonous or otherwise dangerous to humans.

But it was the man he sent in to rape her that led to her finally attempting to escape. She killed the would-be rapist, and when the orderly assigned to her room opened the door to check on the man's screams, she shoved past him and made it down the stairs to the main floor.

Dr. Adams stood in her path to freedom. "Calm down."

Instead, she growled and advanced on him.

He raised a gun. The tranquilizer dart took her out, and she woke with a chain tethered to her ankle that was long enough to allow her to go to the bathroom but not the gym. Unbreakable, she discovered as she fought to snap it.

The doctor let her scream it out for three days. Three days in which she begged and screamed for her wolf to help her.

"Don't bother calling for it," Dr. Adams announced, walking into her room, interrupting her sobbing. "Your monster is gone. I made sure of that."

She blinked at him. "You killed my wolf?"

"Your monster is asleep and will stay that way so long as I'm around." He patted his breast pocket from which a syringe peeked.

"Let me go." Not the first time she'd begged.

"You know I can't do that. What kind of doctor would let a monster like you loose on the world?"

She ran for him, only to have her feet yanked out from under her as the chain snapped taut, jerking her back. She hit the floor hard.

The doctor chuckled. "That will be amusing to watch on replay."

He left. A good thing, because she would have torn him to pieces.

The years after that passed in a blur. The doctor kept her pumped full of drugs, a few that caused strange reactions within her. Partial shifts. Convulsions. She even turned silver for a few hours once.

Why he did it? She couldn't have said. She barely managed to think anymore, having been reduced to an animal who hissed at anyone who showed their face.

Then one day, Dr. Adams entered with his white coat unbuttoned. He appeared more sallow than the last time she'd seen him, and his skin seemed loose, as if he'd lost a lot of weight.

"I hear you're being difficult again." He lectured Luna as if she were simply a recalcitrant child.

Actually, she was a teenager. Possibly a woman by now? She'd lost count of the years she'd been here. Years of torture. Years of being bound. A prisoner. And getting angrier every day.

That anger bubbled especially fiercely at the sight of Dr. Adams. When he'd walked in, something hungry stirred within. Impossible. Dr. Adams had said he'd killed the wolf inside her.

"*Why don't you come closer so we can discuss my attitude?*" She made her smile inviting.

It didn't work.

"*Still trying to scare me after all this time?*" he taunted. "*I'm not afraid of you.*"

"*Says the man who keeps me tied up.*" Chains hung from her wrists, and another wrapped around her ankle.

"*Such a failure you turned out to be.*" The doctor's lips turned down. "*And here I had such high hopes for you.*"

"*So sorry your experiment failed.*" Luna rolled her eyes. What would he do? Punish her?

"*Ungrateful bitch.*" He took a step in her direction and shook his finger.

She wanted to bite it off. "*Big words for a little man.*"

"*You should be thanking me. I took you in when the nuns would have killed you with their rituals.*"

"*You took me in to experiment on me!*"

"*Not in the beginning.*"

"*What about now?*" she pointed out.

"*What I do will help mankind.*"

"*Liar. You do it to help you. A dying man.*" She could smell the truth. The decay grew each time she saw him.

"Fat lot of good that did me. I thought you'd be useful. But instead, you've turned out to be a waste of time."

"If I'm such a disappointment, then set me free."

"Oh, I'll set you free all right," he muttered. As if they'd been signaled, large men flanked him. The orderly to his left regularly held Luna down when they strapped her in for treatment.

Not today.

She backed away, narrowing her gaze. "You're going to kill me." Once, it might have been a relief, but in this moment, she felt only annoyance. The doctor had tortured Luna for years, used her with callous disregard, and now thought he could discard her. Like fuck.

The large men advanced on her. Behind them was a nurse armed with a syringe, already uncapped. Poisons might not have deadly effects, but enough sleeping agent would drop her ass. Just long enough to get her killed.

No.

She hadn't realized she'd whispered aloud until one of the orderlies said, "Don't fight us. This doesn't have to hurt."

Go calmly to her death?

Never.

Luna kept retreating until her back hit a wall. The cold solidity reassured her even as it provided no protection.

The churn within bubbled as they neared, flanking her, readying to pounce.

Set me free. I can save us.

The voice had spoken in her head, a familiar murmur she'd been hearing more and more often of late.

My monster.

The beast inside her was angry and bitter from years of being trapped. It begged Luna to be let go. Promised satisfaction.

The orderlies neared, ready to grab her. The nurse appeared bored as she waited to inject her.

We don't have to die.

But how could Luna set the monster free? The doctor had broken her ability.

You have the power to let me out of my prison.

How?

Relax. Don't fight me.

Why not?

Go ahead. Free us.

The moment she let down her inner shield was when the monster inside surged, hard and fast.

Luna didn't regain her wits until the killing was

done. Crimson rivulets ran down the walls, coated her
skin, drenched her fur. She pushed up on two feet,
which made no sense, given she balanced on paws.

What had happened? Luna staggered over black
and white tile streaked with red. A massive mirror
over a table holding a bowl of flowers caught her
attention.

Actually, the reflection did.

Luna saw a monster. A monster that was—

Me.

Her howl cracked the glass.

NINETEEN

LOCHLAN HELD LUNA TIGHT AS THE NIGHTMARE rocked her. Sweat dewed on her skin, cold and clammy. A tremor shook her from head to toe—her spirit too.

Unlike Luna, Lochlan had no power to see the content of her dream, but he well understood the despair filling her. Remembered its awful taint.

How many nights had he been caught in the thrall of a nightmare? He'd woken too many times, shaking and wet. Terrified to close his eyes. Convinced he wouldn't survive until morning dawned.

In her moments of lonely darkness, he showed her she wasn't alone, because he knew that feeling of abandonment, more than everything, was why so many gave up.

Eventually, her shivering ceased, and she turned so she could press her face to his bare chest. He almost missed her murmured, "I haven't had a bad episode like that in years."

"I imagine it's the stress of confronting the traitor who's messing with you."

"Most likely. But that's not the only thing bugging me," she said with a hot huff against his chest. "What are we going to do if no one will listen?"

On the boat ride over, they'd hashed out a plan. Essentially, they'd find a way to speak to the members of the Lykosium Council Luna thought most likely to be honest. Then they'd expose the rest through a series of tests, until the traitor either got outed or did something to reveal his identity.

"The council would never condone such heinous behavior."

"No, but what if they're afraid or threatened? The traitor appears to have a multitude of minions." Her lips turned down.

"Does he? Or is it money and human nature? At heart, people are followers."

"They're following the orders of a depraved psycho."

"And? It happens. Remember Manson's cult? History is full of examples of people doing stuff they knew was wrong but doing it anyhow because someone told them to."

"Doesn't that contradict your whole 'I don't think the council would condone the traitor's actions'?"

"Let me rephrase, while some might be afraid or blackmailed into support or inaction, I'm going to wager they'd welcome a chance to fight back and rid themselves of the traitor."

"But who can we trust?" she whispered. She had many friends wearing robes. Two dated back to her rescue from the doctor's house. They'd arrived a day too late, but they'd still acted.

"We have to believe that there is a wolf God who is watching and rooting for us to prevail."

She blew a hot snort onto his chest. "Is this where I dumbly say I didn't take you for a religious zealot?"

He smiled against the top of her head. "I'm not, and yet, I believe."

"Even after all that happened to you?"

"Because of it. That helicopter crash? I shouldn't

have survived. That entire day was a series of lucky coincidences. A miracle, if you look at it closely."

"Maybe for you. God wasn't there when I snapped people's necks and ripped out their throats. Reports claim I tore off limbs and flung them around like Frisbees."

"I'll bet they deserved it."

"Doesn't make it right."

"Was it necessary?" was his soft query.

She remained silent for a moment before exhaling a soft, "They hurt me."

The admission killed him, because in that moment, he heard the betrayed little girl. He wanted nothing more than to have saved her. Only, he'd arrived decades too late.

"I'm jealous," he muttered, leading to her surprised exclamation of, "Why?"

"Because you had the guts to take out the people who hurt you. Me? I ran away and hid." He'd often lamented the fact he'd not gone back immediately to rescue his fellow Were. He'd been so afraid he'd get caught and end up stuck in that vicious cycle again. By the time he did act, they'd moved the camp and he never located it again.

"There are times I wish I'd run and hidden from everyone," she said.

"We can still leave," he offered. "Find a remote place, off the grid, just me and you."

"I can't leave Kit."

Relief filled him, as he wasn't sure he could have easily given up his Feral Pack family either. "Then I guess we're finding that traitor."

"Easier said than done," she muttered. "It is tempting to walk away."

"Say the word and I'll whisk you onto a random flight. Then another, until there is no way anyone could follow us. To make sure, once we land, we'll hike under the cover of darkness for at least a few days. Before we resurface, we'll change our appearances, get some new names." He laid out a plan in case she needed a vision.

"You forgot Kit."

"We'll convince him and Poppy to join us."

"She won't leave her brother."

"We'll bring Darian too."

"Why not the whole Feral Pack while we're at it?" was her sarcastic rejoinder.

"I like how you think. We'll relocate somewhere remote, live off the land."

"Sounds like a lot of work," she grumbled.

"Then I guess we're invading a castle."

On their trip, Luna had told him all about the

Lykosium seat of power, their headquarters now for more than a century. The castle could hold a few hundred people easily.

"Why do you sound so exited?" she asked.

"Is this a bad time to mention I've got a secret penchant for historical dramas, especially sieges of castles?"

"We are not laying siege."

"'Course not. We'd need an army for that, or at least a few ballistas. We'll have to enter subtly. Invade from the inside."

Getting in wouldn't be the problem. Leaving alive? That remained uncertain, and yet, they would, because Lochlan hadn't found his mate this late in life only to lose her. Someone was threatening her, which meant Lochlan would ferret them out and handle them.

A train took them to a midsize town in Bulgaria. They arrived without incident. Could be they'd evaded the notice of the traitor, or they were walking into a trap. He guessed the latter.

In town, Luna paid way too much to an old man for an old and rusty car. Lochlan didn't argue with her tense expression. Ever since they'd crossed the border, she'd been focused, firm. Underneath her brave exterior was fear.

A sense of trepidation infected him too. The kind that used to make his mouth dry before a battle. At the same time, it fueled an anticipation that made him hyperalert.

They didn't drive straight up to the castle but, rather, parked at a farm, where they rented some horses for the day. Just a pair of tourists looking to go for a ride.

Luna appeared at ease in the saddle, a woman of many facets, able to adapt to all situations. Always capable and in charge, until they were alone, and then she melted for him. What he wouldn't give to take her away so she never had to deal with any of this ugliness again. She'd suffered enough. But running would mean living in danger. That was all right when it was just his life on the line, but Lochlan wasn't willing to live with hers being threatened.

Rather than ride the horses directly to the castle, she took them on a meandering path that led to a cottage. It was stone on the outside, with a thatched roof from which projected a chimney. No tendrils of smoke escaped despite the sharp bite of cold in the air.

"This place belongs to..." Lochlan racked his brain for a name. Luna had described as many of the

council as she could, though he'd been more interested in memorizing the shape of her body at the
time.

"Padme and Hester, the two oldest council
members. They don't do much anymore, other than
hang out in their garden." By *garden*, did she mean
the one before them? The gate swung loosely in the
breeze. Overripe fruit hung on the plants. More lay
on the ground, rotting. No one had tended this
garden in a while.

A terrible sign that Luna must have seen, and
yet, she didn't remark on it. He said nothing as she
went to the door and rapped sharply, barely waiting
for anyone to answer before opening the door herself
and stepping inside.

The waft of death that emerged kept him
outside, and it was only a moment before she
rejoined him, her face ashen.

No words were needed. Two down. How many
more had already joined Padme and Hester?

They moved on, this time on foot, leaving the
horses behind to graze on the ripe garden. They
didn't speak. They'd said everything that needed to
be said—except for *I love you*.

Lochlan had spent a lifetime avoiding those
words, thinking he didn't deserve them. And now

that he'd found love, he feared losing it. A declaration would have to wait, though. He'd tell her after they prevailed. There would be no *if* about it.

The castle appeared between the trees, the hint of gray stone causing him to tense. Once more, the urge to run hit him hard. *Grab Luna and hide.* But he'd done that once before—hidden—and he'd regretted it. He'd let his brethren down. Let himself down in the process. He'd turned into a bitter old man, a coward who'd let evil flourish because he was afraid.

No more.

They crept quietly on foot even as he thought about shifting to wolf. Which shape would serve him best? As a wolf, he had heightened senses, sharp teeth, and claws. As a man, he had the gun he'd bought from a guy on the street. He had limited ammo—he'd fired it only once to ensure it worked. He could kill more quickly with a weapon. But what about when he ran out of bullets?

The decision got taken from him. The warning, in the form of a quiet too deep and unnatural for the woods, hit him too late.

Bodies dropped from the trees. Silent. Scentless. Aiming too many weapons to avoid.

The perfectly executed ambush had Luna

fuming. Rather than do something foolish, like attack, she held her chin high. "Stand down. I am with the council."

"On your knees, hands over your head," a voice barked, the person's features hidden by a dark mask.

"Do you know who I am?" Spoken in Luna's haughtiest tone.

"Indeed, I do. I know you better than you know yourself, Luna." A robed figure appeared, stepping from behind a massive trunk. His scent was familiar somehow, bringing a frown to Lochlan's brow.

"Peter." Luna said the name flatly. "I should have guessed you would be the traitor. Although I admit I'm surprised you had time to ferment betrayal between your whoring and gambling."

"Here we go again. The saintly Luna, lecturing me about behavior unbecoming a council member," the robed figure taunted.

That voice nagged at Lochlan.

"You should have never been inducted into the council," she said. "I'm going to guess you blackmailed your way into a spot."

"Hardly necessary when bribery works much better."

"You won't get away with this. Most of the council hates you."

"They did. Which is why they had to go. You know what they say—out with the old, in with the new."

"You killed them all?" She couldn't hide her shock.

"Not all. Only those who should have stepped down long ago and didn't take well to change."

"And you're going to kill me next?" She remained defiant and brave.

"What a waste that would be of your genetics."

"Whatever your diabolical plot, I won't help."

"You won't have a choice. You and the AWOL soldier by your side are now in my power."

Only as the man peeled back his hood did Lochlan gasp. "Sergeant McLean?"

TWENTY

THE SHOCK OF HEARING LOCHLAN CALL PETER by another name didn't have time to sink in, not with Peter barking out commands.

"Put the male in a cage. Try not to kill him, though. I know Dr. Itranj will be excited to see the lost corporal."

The threat led to Lochlan snapping, "Like fuck!"

He pulled his gun and fired rapidly. The bullets missed Peter but did hit two soldiers in the chest, but to little effect, given they wore body armor.

Lochlan didn't have the same protection. Darts peppered his chest. Swaying and trying to stay awake, he slurred, "I'm sorry, sweetheart."

He was sorry? It was her fault they'd gotten caught in a trap. She'd not expected the traitor to gain control of the Lykosium so thoroughly. Yet another miscalculation. A deadly one.

Lochlan slumped before falling over, and as much as she wanted to rush to his aid, she knew she could offer him little help. She should have brought a weapon.

You are a weapon. Her monster pulsed. *Let me out.*

As if she'd listen. She couldn't afford to be out of her mind. Especially when it would accomplish nothing. The soldiers would have her snoring on the ground before she could shred her clothes.

"Shall we?" Peter indicated the path before him, but rather than walk behind her, he kept pace while his flanking soldiers ensured she couldn't escape. As if she'd leave Lochlan, being carried behind them, unconscious and vulnerable. He needed her to find a way out of this mess. That started with information.

"You and Lochlan know each other," she stated.

"He served under me when I was playing the part of Sergeant McLean."

She cocked her head as she eyed him. The version of Peter she'd briefly seen in Lochlan's dream had had him clean-shaven and short-haired—in other words, unrecognizable. The Peter she knew had always sported long, shaggy hair and a beard. "Playing the part?"

"As if I ever wanted to fight for anyone but myself."

"You were an enforcer when I met you." The one and only time she'd seen him, he'd been with Padme during her rescue.

"A job that turned out to be boring, so I moved on to more challenging things. Turns out humans are as easy to manipulate as Were. With the right leverage, it's easy to rise in rank."

What he implied hit her like a slap. "You're the one who betrayed the Were to the human military."

"Yes and no. The military was already aware of the Were. What they didn't have was a means to pick them out among the human grunts."

"You helped them?" She almost yelled, wondering why none of the men around them reacted. How could they not care about such betrayal of their kind?

A glance to the side showed the guards staring ahead. Uninterested.

"Don't bother with them. They know better than to betray me. They've seen what happens."

Given Peter's propensity for killing, she could guess what kind of threats he used.

"You've been murdering our people."

"Our people?" Peter snorted. "Gutless animals content with scraps when we should be ruling the world."

"We hide to protect ourselves."

"We hide because those in charge lack courage and vision. I am meant for better things than that, and so are you, *sister*."

A roaring filled her head at the word. "Don't say that. We're not related."

"Actually, we are. Same mother, same father. I'm two years older than you. I was the one left behind when our mother fled with her darling baby, leaving me with *him*." His voice dropped an octave.

"I don't understand." Luna truly didn't. She'd been only a child when her mother had dragged her around the country. She'd been too young to grasp why, and later in life, she'd assumed her mother had been hiding from something—or someone.

"Let's just say Father had a bit of a temper. Use your imagination, and I'm sure you can figure out the rest."

Spousal abuse would explain why her mother had run away. "I'm sorry she left you behind."

He laughed. "I'm not. Better to be raised by

someone strong than weak. I learned much during those years after her abandonment."

"What happened to..." She couldn't say father, but Peter understood.

"He died when I no longer had a use for him. I swear his eyes glinted with pride when I ended his life."

Was Peter always this depraved? Had that been why her mother left him behind?

"What does any of this have to do with you betraying the Were to that psycho Gerard Kline and the military?"

"Nothing. That was purely business. The council doesn't pay its members very well. Always putting their donations and funds toward protecting the Were, blah, blah, blah," Peter complained as they exited the forest and beheld the massive, looming castle. "A man like me needs more. So I struck deals everywhere I could. The military, the rich, even your precious council members have a price. The result paid off, and I moved up in the Lykosium ranks."

"Through lies and subterfuge? There's no way someone didn't catch on to you."

"It's amazing how easy it is to bury unfortunate information, like the disappearance of a few Were here and there."

"A few? Your actions annihilated entire Packs."

"A mistake, given the acceleration of my actions drew unfortunate attention. I should have stuck with a few from each Pack here and there to hide it better."

His nonchalance stunned her. "You're a murderer."

"And?" He showed absolutely no remorse.

"I don't care if we're related. I will kill you."

"How? We both know you don't shift. Not without some help, that is." He sneered. "Dr. Adams sure did a number on you with his experiments. Pity you had to go and kill him."

She blinked. "The man tortured me."

"Dr. Adams was a visionary. A search of his house proved to be an eye-opener. Did you know about his many journals detailing every step of his studies?"

"You've seen his notes?" She'd assumed they'd burned with his house. She'd stood with Padme, the one leading the charge to rescue her that day, and watched the dancing flames as they'd eradicated her prison. Pity the fire couldn't cleanse her memories.

"Adams wrote about you and the ones that came before you. He had so many journals that detailed his experiments and studies. Given Padme and her gang weren't the type to appreciate his work, I buried the lot in the woods until I could return for them at a later date. Which turned out to be almost a year, and then it took me a while to read through all the science mumbo jumbo that I didn't have time to learn. I wasn't a very patient man in those days. Nor a rich one. That's why the military proved useful. They had the people who could decipher Adams' work and could help me perfect some of his serums. At the same time, they proved restrictive, complaining about budgets and how hard it was to hide the deaths of the soldiers we drafted into the program. I hooked up with Kline after that. He provided the funds to continue Dr. Adams' studies, which were, coincidentally, on a girl with the same name as the sister I'd lost."

"Studies." She blew out the word with disdain, even as she absorbed just how long he'd been betraying the Were. So many lives lost because of him. And he didn't care.

"You should be proud of the contributions you made to his research," Peter said. "Because of you, Adams saw the Were condition as something to be controlled and created the tools to do so, such as the formulas to suppress or force shifting."

The blatant revelation had her snapping, "By

giving Kline those powders, you tortured and murdered your own people."

"Giving?" Peter laughed. "I'm not a charity. Kline paid a fortune for each and every package."

The perfidy never ended, and it also came full circle. Dr. Adams might have died the day Luna had escaped, but it appeared his evil legacy lived on in Peter. It almost pained her to ask, "Are you Kit's father?" Might as well get all the answers she could before she killed him.

Because she would, even if it was the last thing she did.

"Kit. What a stupid name."

"We like it." She defended the nickname that had stuck. It wasn't as if Kit were a rare appellation among humans. Plenty of guys had that name. "You didn't answer the question."

"I donated sperm to the vixen who birthed him. For a Kitsune, Mariella was very fecund but not very obedient. She got angry when she found out I had a buyer for our first litter."

"You sold your own children?" Luna still had the capacity to be shocked. "I thought she and the children were captured."

"They were. Kline preferred a bit of sport. I sold

him a location that just happened to have what he was looking for."

Luna swayed on her feet. "What kind of depraved asshole sells his own family as fodder for hunters?"

"I told you, I needed funding."

"Bastard." She couldn't help but lunge for him.

Her hands never made it around his throat.

Tranquilizer darts hit her from all sides, the stings barely registering, but the drugs dropped her straight into darkness.

She woke in a cage.

TWENTY-ONE

LOCHLAN WAS LOCKED IN A CAGE, AND IT WAS his own fault. He and Luna had walked right into a trap. He'd seen it coming a mile away, and he hadn't fucking dodged it. He should have whisked Luna away the moment they'd discovered the council members in that cottage had been murdered.

Not that she would have let him. The woman wasn't the type to shirk her responsibility, no matter the danger. Even when they were surrounded, she'd held her head high.

Damn her confident and sexy ass.

Lochlan lacked the same cool composure. Just look at his reaction when he'd seen his old sergeant, the fucker who'd betrayed him and so many others. He would have liked nothing more than to tear off

Sergeant McLean's face and feed it to him. However, he'd failed. The soldiers armed with tranqs had taken him out before he could do any real damage.

Sedative missiles, not bullets, had dropped Lochlan. Good and bad news. The good? He'd lived. The bad? McLean wanted him alive, which meant he had something planned. As the sedatives had hit, Lochlan had had a choice—fight and lose because he had no advantage or feign being knocked out. He'd figured he might have a better chance at escape later.

Would McLean remember Lochlan's resistance to most drugs? Hopefully not.

Lochlan had let his limbs go limp and hit the ground, eyes shut, faking unconsciousness. Let them buy the act. He would wait and watch for the right opportunity. It was the best way to help Luna.

She'd remained poised, at least to those who didn't know her. But Lochlan knew her better than he knew himself. He'd sensed the simmering emotion within her. Anger at the situation, more at the betrayal. As for fear? She'd used her ire to keep it at bay. But he'd known it was there.

She needed Lochlan.

Needed him to be smart.

Much as he'd wanted to rush to the rescue, he'd willed himself to remain noodlelike as the scentless soldiers had grabbed him by the arms and dragged him into the castle.

They hadn't been gentle about his transport, thumping him down some steps with no care about bruising or breaking anything. The stairs must have been original to the castle, given the smoothness of the stone, hollowed in the middle from all the foot traffic.

A door at the bottom led them into a large, circular chamber that hammered him with scents. The antiseptic smell of a hospital, a chemical clean that irritated the nose. Despite the overpowering ammonia, the scents of urine, blood, and panic lingered.

The soldiers holding him on either side had headed for a cage and thrown him in, dropping him to the concrete floor face first.

As the door to the cage had clanked shut, one of them had complained, "Hate these coats. They're made too small."

"Only if you tell them the wrong size," the other soldier riposted and laughed.

A zipper went down as the lock clicked.

"I don't even know why they make us wear them. We could just spray our clothes with that stuff that makes us invisible."

As the scents of the humans had come to Lochlan, it had taken everything in him not to react. Because he'd been caught by humans. The old sergeant had aligned himself with the Were's greatest enemy.

At the receding steps of the soldiers, he cracked open an eye to check his situation. The cage had a concrete floor, smooth but for a small hole—the kind meant to drain bodily fluids after torture. By the smell, it had been used plenty. Blood, sweat, and terror seemed to ooze from the walls and floor of the refurbished dungeon.

He remained lying still, listening as he eyed the bars of the cage that were made from some kind of metal coated with silver. What a joke. Only the truly superstitious screamed that they burned at the touch of silver.

As the door to the dungeon shut behind the soldiers, he opened both eyes, only to startle at the sight of a watcher.

Gaunter than Lochlan recalled, Dr. Itranj hadn't aged well in the decade or so since Lochlan had escaped. The man had also hidden his scent so thoroughly a sluggish Lochlan had not suspected he was near.

Someone really needed to destroy that formula, because a Were's sense of smell was everything.

"I knew you weren't dead." Itranj beamed, his expression that of a delighted child at Christmas.

It was gross to see a grown man so excited by the prospect of torture, but not really surprising.

"I see no one has torn you apart yet. Shame," was his dry reply.

"Still sarcastic, indicating your cognitive abilities haven't degraded." Already, the man analyzed him. Itranj moved around the cage.

Lochlan rose and spun to keep him in sight.

"You appear in decent shape," Itranj remarked.

"Unlike you." The doctor's shoulders hunched, and he looked too thin, in contrast to his previously plump girth.

Itranj ignored his words to murmur some more observations. "Seems as if you are still resistant to sleeping agents. What of poisons?"

"I usually avoid those. They tend to make me feel bloated," Lochlan drawled. The last part was true, but he didn't avoid them. On the contrary, one thing Lochlan had ensured during his hiding years was that he remained as tough or tougher than when he'd served. He'd usually done that alone, sweating through the effects over and over until he'd mastered the ailment.

"It will be interesting to compare your test results with those in the control group."

The doctor's statement froze him. "What control group?"

"The one McLean acquired for me. It was one of my requests to us partnering again."

"You haven't been working with him this entire time?"

"Kind of hard, given we served in different prisons."

"You went to jail?"

"Old charges from my time in Europe before I learned the people weren't ready for my greatness."

"How did you and McLean end up working together again?" Lochlan asked, fascinated despite himself.

"He contacted me, actually. Wanted to know if I'd made any advances since we parted. I would have if I'd been given access to some subjects. Now I have more than enough to finish my work." Itranj rubbed his hands together in glee.

"You captured some Were?"

"McLean and his people did. Initially, he wanted to kill everyone in the castle, but I advised him it would be a foolish waste. Instead, we put suitable candidates to sleep and relocated them to the holding cells." He waved to an open door on the far side of the dungeon that led to a corridor filled with small rooms whose doors could be barred from the outside.

Luna had described this dungeon to him and had also somberly explained that no one had ever escaped from it. He intended to win against those odds.

He eyed the room more closely, realizing that the new concrete floor and silver cage weren't the only recent changes. The ancient torture devices had been replaced with ones used in modern medicine that lit up and beeped. Vials were lined up, waiting for fluids.

His gaze returned to the far door, and he imagined the Were imprisoned behind all those barred doors. They would be allies if he could free them.

Lochlan stalled Itranj by talking some more. He rose and asked, "What exactly are you trying to accomplish?"

"Everything," Itranj declared. "The lycanthropic gene that is active in you and the others will open up the door to all kinds of things."

"Like? Because I was with you for a long fucking time, and the only thing you ever accomplished was an ability to kill good folk."

Itranj pursed his lips. "I'll admit there have been some setbacks. But that was because I was hamstrung by the colonel and the military. Now, I can do anything I'd like."

Words to give even the bravest person chills.

The conversation stalled as booted feet approached, tromping without care down the steps.

The hairs on his body lifted. The soldiers hadn't come alone.

They entered carrying Luna, more carefully than they'd dragged him. Itranj practically ran to open the other cage for them.

Oh no.

Oh fucking hell no.

"Get away from her," he couldn't help but growl.

Itranj ignored him and clapped his hands. "At last, Subject Zero." The man practically orgasmed in delight.

"She has a name," Lochlan muttered. As if Itranj cared. He was too busy hovering over Luna, drooling.

Lochlan grabbed the metal bars and burned. Not from the silver but from the cold rage inside him. Funny how he'd never been this angry about the things that had been done to him.

Experiment on me, shame on me.

Touch a hair on Luna, and you die.

Itranj clasped his hands and whispered, "Do you know special she is? Do you know that Subject Zero is the only one who's gone through all of Adams' experiments and survived? I've never been able to replicate those results. Although you came close." He slewed a gaze over his shoulder at Lochlan. "I wonder if you'd survive the last few tests, like she did."

"Why don't you come close and try?" Lochlan beckoned.

"I can't wait to break that spirit. I learned some things in prison. Ways to hurt that I never imagined. Would you like me to show you?" He giggle.

The threat was seriously the scariest shit Lochlan had ever heard. And that served only to increase his rage. Because that man planned to hurt Luna.

"If you're so keen on experiments, why not try some of the needles on yourself? Maybe you'll become The Hulk of the wolf world."

"If only it worked that way." Itranj's lips turned down. "I can't get anything to work the way I want it to. Damned weaklings keep dying." The man sounded so sad.

So sick.

Lochlan had to get Luna away from here. "Why would you consider Luna a success? She can't shift." He lied to protect her.

"Not entirely true," sang the doctor, wagging his finger. "According to McLean, she will shift with the forced-shift powder. Not into a wolf but into some hybrid version. An interesting side effect that's never happened with the other subjects."

"Those subjects were people." Lochlan knew his words wouldn't make a dent. However, the longer he distracted Itranj, the more the drugs in his system, and Luna's, would dissipate. He no longer felt sluggish.

Itranj didn't reply for a long moment then said, "I think I'll start by analyzing her blood. I want a baseline for comparison. Then I'll do a physical exam to check for differences. I hear she's developed some interesting eyes." The doctor turned to face Lochlan. "Did you know McLean didn't tell me about her existence until recently? To think years have been wasted because he felt some oddly misplaced loyalty toward his sister."

"Wait, they're related?"

"Yes. Apparently, the parents separated, and each one took a child. Luna ended up in the care of Dr. Adams. And in a stroke of luck, her brother was one of those who found her. His mistake was in ignoring her. He thought her defective, when, in reality, she is the perfect answer."

The news of Luna being related to the sergeant rocked Lochlan. He could only imagine what that information had done to Luna. "Better not hurt her, then, or McLean will be pissed."

Itranj snorted. "McLean is dedicated to the cause. He doesn't care if she's related. She's useful now. That's why he finally handed her over."

"What cause is he working for?" he asked, focusing on the first part.

"There is only one cause worth my time, and that's the one that makes me richer." The sergeant walked into the room and smiled at Lochlan. "Hello again, Corporal. I trust you and the doctor are having a nice reunion."

"You fucker." He couldn't help but seethe.

McLean had changed since Lochlan had known him. For one, he'd grown out the hair on his head and his face, which had changed the contour of his head. He wore a turtleneck sweater and pleated slacks, having ditched the robe from earlier. Based on looks alone, Lochlan would have never recognized him as the same man who'd led to his torture in the military. But his scent didn't lie.

"Is that how you want to speak to me, given your situation?" McLean arched a brow.

"It's how I talk to a traitor," Lochlan spat.

"I prefer the term 'wealthy man.'"

"Soon to be a dead one."

"By whose hands?" McLean mocked. "There is no one left to fight me. I executed the perfect coup. Took the entire Lykosium Council and their staff prisoner. Except for the old ones. I had no use for them."

"How? The enforcers should have stopped you."

"I handled them first. It wasn't that hard, given we are at our all-time lowest numbers. I spread them out on multiple missions that weren't really missions, if you know what I mean." McLean smirked.

He'd ambushed them all... Luna had pegged it right when she'd called him evil. Sergeant Peter McLean was the kind of evil that had to be stopped.

"You won't get away with it."

"I already have."

"Don't be so sure of that."

McLean laughed. "That's priceless coming from a man in a cage."

"You really think this will hold me?" Lochlan stroked the bars.

"That silver is just a thin layer over the steel rods. Even you can't bend those."

"Let's say, for shits and giggles, I can. Do you want to die quickly or slowly? Please say slowly. I'm pretty sure I'll enjoy hearing you scream."

"You're vastly outnumbered."

Lochlan's lip curled. "You talking about the humans you've surrounded yourself with? How much do you have to pay them to obey you?"

"I hired them because the Were are too squeamish to act."

"I would have said it's because no one wants to support a murdering psycho."

"You call it murder, and yet, I'm sure Dr. Itranj would call it progress."

The doctor, kneeling by Luna's cage, had extended her arm through the bars so he could draw blood.

Luna's eyes shot open.

Fear filled them.

Despair.

She was a little girl about to suffer once more.

No.

Lochlan gripped the bars tighter. They creaked.

McLean's eyes widened before narrowing. "Go

ahead and strain. You can't break the cage holding you."

"I'll take that wager," Lochlan drawled. He flexed his arms, testing the strength of the bars, wondering how deep into the concrete they went, how much he'd have to bend and where to gain some leverage.

"You are awfully desperate to get out. Is this because of my sister?" McLean pretended to grab his heart and chuckled. "Is it true? Did she finally find her mate? A man she'll do anything for?"

"You shouldn't be mocking it, McLean," Lochlan stated softly. "Interesting thing about man, or beast. When it comes to strength, it's not size or muscle that counts, but want. Need." Metal groaned as his arms bulged, his skin sprouting hairs as he strained.

"How are you doing that?" McLean breathed, backing away.

Itranj had the same question as he neared. "He shouldn't be able to shift. The tranquilizers had the impeding compound."

"Now, now, boys, did you really think I'd gotten weaker during our separation?" Lochlan's voice held a low timbre as his jaw changed shape and his canines lengthened. "I've been waiting for this day. Wanna see a trick I learned after I quit the military?"

The effects of the drugs had worn off, and Lochlan shifted. Not into a wolf who would be useless in this cage. He shifted into something he'd only ever done in private before. A hybrid. Part wolf, part man. With hands to grip and the strength of many wolves. He had the added benefit of the adrenaline that came from knowing his mate was in danger.

With a howl and a burst of power, he wrenched the bars, bending them enough that they loosened in the concrete. He twisted and pulled, putting his weight into it.

They popped out, leaving a body-sized gap.

He offered the jaw-dropped Itranj and shocked McLean a toothy grin.

Then lunged.

TWENTY-TWO

THE SCREAM OF METAL BENDING IN UNNATURAL ways had Luna blinking. She thought blurry vision was to blame for what looked like bars in front of her eyes.

But no, she realized, she was in a cage.

And across from her, in another cell, was Lochlan. Not the man she knew, though, or even the wolf she'd met. A two-legged wolfman wearing Hulk-tattered jeans and a straining T-shirt wrenched apart the bars of his cage and pulled them free of the concrete.

Lochlan's wolfish grin led to strident yelling from a little old man in a white coat while someone whirled and ran.

"Stay in that cage or else!" the white-coated human yelled.

"Or else what, Itranj?" growled Beast Lochlan as he stepped through the gap he'd made.

"Sound the alarm. Breach! Breach!" The last part was shrieked as the little man ran for a table laden with vials and syringes. He grabbed one and whirled just as Lochlan surged toward him with a roar.

Itranj—a name familiar to her because of the stories she and Lochlan had exchanged on their long ocean voyage—jabbed. The needle sank into Lochlan's flesh.

For a moment, Itranj had a ridiculous wet-lipped smirk on his face. That faded as Lochlan pulled the syringe free, dropped it, and then shook his finger and head as he tsked. "Bad."

Luna almost laughed as the man freaked out. There was nothing funny about the situation.

She crawled to the bars of her cage and held on to them, only belatedly realizing she'd licked her lips when Lochlan slashed a paw across the doctor's throat. The man in the white coat, the sadistic bastard who'd once tortured him, sank to his knees, fingers clutching in a vain attempt to stem the gushing blood.

Itranj was dead, even if he'd yet to acknowledge it. The bleed-out didn't take long. The doctor fell over, and Lochlan's head swiveled in her direction. He grinned with too many teeth, two of them extra long, and managed to huff, "Out?"

How could he speak in such a shape? She nodded. "Please."

He strode toward her, a magnificent specimen, muscled and yet furry, lean-hipped and long-legged. His hairy fingers ending in claws. A dichotomy of parts.

A monster like me.

And yet, he didn't seem like a monster. He grabbed hold of her bars and wrenched them apart, his arms bulging as he strained.

She placed her hand on a bicep and then eyed him, a strange longing inside her. Why couldn't her monster be this beautiful?

Am beautiful. Why won't you see it?

Her lips parted, but before she could say a word, soldiers poured into the room, firing weapons filled with tranqs rather than bullets, or things would have been really dire.

The heroic type, Lochlan threw himself in front of her, taking the brunt of the missiles. He roared as he yanked a handful out before charging the soldiers.

Mighty swings of his arms scattered the humans, though that only delayed their deaths. One by one, Lochlan tore them apart, literally. Arms were ripped off and tossed. Necks were twisted and snapped. Entrails spilled to the floor. She should have been appalled. A normal person would have looked away. But instead, she couldn't help but admire, even as she'd hated herself for doing the same.

When the soldiers were dead, or shortly on their way to dying, Lochlan returned to her side, sweating and panting.

"McLean sent them. Fucker ran." It wasn't just his hybrid shape distorting his words this time. The sleeping drug was racing through his system.

"We have to get him." The traitor couldn't be allowed to escape.

Lochlan dropped to a knee, bowed his head. "Need. Minute." The words slurred from his muzzle.

She stroked his hair. "You should have let a few of those hit me."

"No." A harsh exclamation. "No hurt. Mate."

"Oh, Lochlan." His insistence on protecting her squeezed her heart. Which was why it was so hard to say, "You take that minute to recover. I have to go after Peter."

"No." The syllable roused him for a second.

"I have to. He can't escape."

"Give. Second," Lochlan mumbled, his eyes shutting. They didn't reopen. His body went limp against her.

She eased him to the floor, wincing at the amount of darts that jutted from his body. He'd received a large amount of drugs at once. He wouldn't wake for a while.

She kissed his mouth and whispered, "I love you." The first time she'd ever said that to a lover.

Probably the last time too.

Despite hating how vulnerable it left Lochlan, she hustled out of the dungeon, not wanting to lose Peter's trail. She grabbed two of the tranquilizer guns on the way. *Let's see how he likes waking up in a cage.*

She took the stairs two at a time, expecting at any moment to run into more soldiers. She learned soon enough that they waited for her on the main floor—their smell gave them away. Rather than exit the dungeon where they would expect, she got the drop on them from above. Having the advantage of knowing every nook and cranny of the castle, including its secret passageways, she emerged on a dusty balcony that was almost a Juliet, given its small size, and started firing.

But the guns had only a few medicinal shots each, enough to down four of the seven remaining soldiers. That left three humans. Easy for a wolf to handle, but Luna's was shut away.

Let me out.

How? She didn't have any drugs to help. She ducked back into the passageway and made her way to a closet close to the castle's entrance. She emerged to see the backs of the three remaining soldiers as they eyed the second floor that ringed the front hall.

Watch out.

The warning came too late.

Hands grabbed her from behind, clamping around her throat and yanking her off her feet. The lack of scent had tricked her, and she wanted to curse the drugs that still hadn't cleared her system and dulled her senses.

Let me out.

The lack of air caused spots to dance in her eyes.

I can't. I don't know how.

Let go. Trust me. For I am you.

As her body started to twitch, she had no choice but to die or give up control. It wasn't easy to close her eyes and let go. She tensed, remembering all the pain she'd suffered, the name-calling, the terror.

"This will hurt. Go ahead and scream, monster."

"Filthy animal."

"Don't cry, or I'll really give you a reason."

They called her monster because, when she shifted, she truly became one. It was such a blessing to not remember the things she did.

As her monster surged, she expected to get shoved into that dark room that kept her ignorant until she woke up with a mouth filled with coppery blood. But this time, she was aware. She felt her body changing and had a nostalgic moment in which she remembered being a wolf rather than a monster.

As she shifted, Peter startled, and his grip slipped. He jerked back when she snapped at him, full-muzzled and shaggy-furred. On four legs, Luna the wolf eyed her enemy and snarled.

The coward pulled a gun and aimed it. "Back off."

She huffed and scuffed a paw. A human wouldn't have understood the shade she'd thrown. But Peter did.

"You dare challenge me? It's time I showed you your place, *sister*." He set his gun aside and stripped off his shoes and shirt before he shifted into a deep gray wolf, a true contrast to her bright silver. He loomed larger than her but that was the only difference, and it didn't stop her charge. She dove for the brother she'd just found, determined to become an only child once more. She had no thought other than killing this blight upon the world. How one person could be so evil and destroy so many lives boggled the mind.

It ended now.

As they slammed into each other, two beasts of fur and fang, they grunted and heaved from the hall by the closet into the main corridor. The remaining humans watched, aiming their weapons but getting no clear shot.

That didn't stop one of them from firing—and hitting Peter. He snapped and shoved away from Luna, grabbing the dart with his teeth and yanking it free. When he roared in the direction of his soldiers, they dropped their weapons and ran.

Peter turned on her, head low, his growl menacing. Her gaze went to the gun he'd eschewed, only a few paces away. A gun she couldn't use because of her paws.

She didn't avoid his lunge but met it, grunting at the impact of his body hitting hers. They snapped and snarled, rolling on the floor.

The tussle resulted with him on top of her, and his mouth grabbed hold of her neck. She couldn't shove him off with her flailing paws. She didn't even think, just half shifted, shoving at his head, trying to prevent him from crushing her neck.

She shoved him from her and crouched as he prepared to lunge once more. Her hairy hand slapped down on top of the gun she'd managed to get close to, and she lifted it as he soared through the air toward her.

Bang.

She shot him between the eyes. And just in case... *Bang.* She shot him in the heart too.

This time, when she melted back into her human shape, blood dripping from her nose and glossing her lips, she remembered everything.

And cried.

TWENTY-THREE

LOCHLAN FOUND LUNA SOBBING BESIDE THE
body of the sergeant.

"Sweetheart, are you hurt?" He skidded to his
knees, uncaring of the resulting burn.

"I'm fine." She sniffled as she rubbed a hand over
her bloody nose. "Just relieved. It's over."

He glanced at the very dead sergeant. Her
brother and the man behind just about everything.
With him and Itranj gone, Lochlan and Luna had a
chance of fixing things.

"I'm sorry it took me so long to get here." He'd
had to metabolize the sleeping agent and even now
struggled against the anti-shifting chemicals still
invading his blood. He'd thought to release the

imprisoned Lykosium as allies, only to react in horror upon discovering everyone in those cells dead. The chips inside them had been detonated. One final horrific act by the desperate sergeant.

Luna reached for him, and he gathered her into his arms, rocking her in his grasp. His fear when he'd woken to find her gone...He never wanted to deal with that again.

"We have to go back down there," she whispered against his skin. "Maybe there are survivors."

He heaved a shaky breath before telling her then held her anew as she wailed. They'd failed to save them, a guilt they'd have to live with, tempered only slightly by the evidence she found in McLean's room that showed more than a few who'd died had abetted him, or hadn't cared enough to try to stop a madman.

Later, they watched as the castle burned, not an easy thing to accomplish when the place was constructed of stone. It had taken all the gas they could siphon from the cars in the garage to get the nightmare dungeon to burn properly. The police might find bodies, but they'd never know what had happened or be able to identify them.

They set off on foot with only the supplies they could carry, heading back to Padme and Hester's cabin, hoping the horses had stuck around. They hadn't, but neither did they.

It took a while before Luna chose to speak, and when she did, what she said didn't surprise him. "You never told me you were a hybrid wolf like me."

That lifted the corner of his lip. "I wouldn't say 'like you.' My junk is a tad different, don't you think?"

She smacked him. "Don't joke. You know what I mean. You stood on two legs and had great big fangs."

"Yup."

"On purpose."

"Yep."

"How come—"

"I never told you? Because, despite all kinds of practice, I'm not always able to do it on demand."

"Why would you want to be a monster?"

"First off, not a monster. Just a different extension of me. Sometimes I run on four paws. Sometimes on two feet. And when the need calls for it, I blend the two. Just like you can."

She shook her head. "Not like me. I'm broken."

"Are you, or did you let those nuns and doctor and humans get in your head? Personally, I think it's your subconscious fucking with you. Those fuckers made you believe shifting was evil."

"Because it's violent."

"Violent with who? I'll tell you—people who would hurt you. It defended you. Ever think of trusting it?"

She paused for a moment before replying, "Today, no drugs were required to let it out, and I remember everything."

"For once, you were allies, not enemies. As it should be. As it will be from now on."

She sighed. "What if it was a one-time deal? I don't know if I can risk letting it loose again only to find out I'm wrong."

"Then I guess Adams wins."

"Adams is dead."

"He is, and yet, you want to persist in believing you can't be whole."

"I don't know how," she whispered.

"Neither do I, but I think we'll be able to find out together. Which reminds me, you said something earlier. Something about love." He'd been drifting into la-la land when he'd heard her whisper the words.

Her cheeks turned pink. "Don't know what you're talking about." She wouldn't look at him.

He tilted her chin. "You want me to say it first, then I will. I love you, Luna Smith. Mate. Lover. What do you say we go home?"

And by *home*, there was only one place he meant.

EPILOGUE

Mud sprayed in a filthy arc as Luna plowed through a watery patch. The wheels of her quad spun and spat dirt at the person riding her tail.

She leaned low and gunned the machine hard, uttering a cry of joy as she and the ATV, on four wheels instead of paws, flew up the incline and then popped over the rim, momentarily weightless.

"Woo-hoo!" she yodeled.

The man at her back echoed the cry.

Her mate.

The ATV hit the ground, and the tires slid before gripping. Off she sped, having the time of her life.

She'd been at White Wolf Ranch, the home of the Feral Pack, for a week now and loved it. Funnily enough, when she'd come for a visit with Lochlan to figure things out now that the Lykosium had been virtually wiped out, she'd expected to be bored. Usually, she got fidgety when she spent too long in one place. She'd certainly never expected to actually enjoy simple country living, given her most recent residence was literally a castle with every amenity at her fingertips.

Amarok proved to be the right kind of Alpha, kind and caring but firm, with a Pack who supported one another like family.

A family that was bigger now that Astra had birthed her baby—a girl who Bellamy boasted was the most beautiful child ever.

They all agreed. Even Luna, who'd offered to walk with the child a few nights, basking in the smell of a baby. Not something she'd experienced before, and at this point in her life, starting a baby from scratch didn't appeal to her, but she did love that powder-fresh scent.

There were lots of things to like about White Wolf Ranch. It had all the comforts she needed. Bed. Bathroom with hot water. A kitchen, though that apparently lacked the usually delicious meals because Poppy was still honeymooning with Kit— and the children.

It pleased Luna to no end to know he'd told Poppy his secret and taken her to meet the children he fostered. No surprise, Poppy had fallen in love with them all. She'd even been willing to uproot and move in with them then and there, only Kit had had a taste of the ranch life. Poppy didn't know it yet, but he'd made an offer on the property practically adjoining Amarok's. It held a large farmhouse, two smaller bungalows, and several outbuildings. Room to grow.

Not that Kit planned to become a farmer. However, with the Lykosium having been dismantled, he did have to find a new purpose.

As for Luna's new job?

Nothing.

For the first time in forever, she had not one fucking thing to do.

She'd saved enough over the years that she could buy what she needed, which had turned out to be less than she'd imagined. As a matter of fact, she didn't need a single material thing so long as she could have the man riding by her side.

She stopped at the end of a perfect grassy field atop a knoll that managed to evade the shadow of the trees. A perfect place for lovers.

Before she could slide off her machine, Lochlan

was grabbing her—he liked to carry her, said he needed to do it to keep in shape. She knew it had more to do with reassuring himself she was safe. After all they'd been through, it didn't surprise her that sometimes the nightmares tried to drag them down. The nightmares could try, but they wouldn't win, because she and Lochlan had found each other. Together, they could face anything.

Luna nuzzled her mate. "It's a full moon tonight," she mentioned as he laid her down on the ground, the warm grass fragrant beneath her.

"You trying to tell me something?"

"I think I'd like to try."

"Are you sure?" he asked.

She nodded. It was time to reunite with her wolf. Not the monster. Not the beast. Not her curse.

Because, it turned out, she was always the one in control; she just hadn't known it. She chose her shape. She could choose to be undivided. Whole.

That night, when the moon's silver rays tickled her naked skin, she let the change sweep over her, a thing of beauty and exultation. Not fear. Not pain.

She howled with joy. Her mate ululated alongside her.

Let's run.

So they did, two rogues unloved, finally at peace and accepted.

Awoo!

The end of the Feral Pack series. For now. You never know when I'll get an idea. After all, not all of them have found their mate.

For more info on this book or more Eve Langlais titles, please visit, EveLanglais.com.

CPSIA information can be obtained
at www.ICGtesting.com
Printed in the USA
LVHW091405051222
734608LV00017B/1516

9 781773 843131